Twilight's Last Gleaming

Spangled Banner Series

Book One

Twilight's Last Gleaming
By T. Brady and J. Del Monte
© 2006

A **Write Up The Road** Book

For more information contact:
Write Up The Road Publishing
P.O. Box 69
Kenton, TN 38233
(800) 292-8072
www.writeuptheroad.com

Twilight's Last Gleaming
Brady, T. and Del Monte, J.
ISBN: 0-9724026-2-4
LCCN: 2005907095

Cover design by Write Up The Road
Printed in the United States of America

Dedication

*To all American truckers ...
and our troops.*

Before Twilight

The old man sat quietly on a park bench after he'd eaten the thin sandwich of potted meat, waiting to see if the even thinner stray cat would show up. It was a chilly day; he had on a worn overcoat, buttoned tightly, with a scarf tucked around his neck. Passers-by didn't see him; he was just another New Yorker seated in the park. Held carefully in his fingers was a scrap of his sandwich, saved for the black cat with amber eyes. He'd wait. Seth Garner had nothing else to do.

Maybe he dozed a little as he sat there; Seth was never quite sure how long he waited that day in late March. A sharp pain in the calf of his right leg; he must've bent his knee too much and the poor circulation made it hurt. He tentatively stretched the muscles just a little. The cat wrapped herself around his ankles, anxious for the treat. He handed the sandwich scrap to the animal, which gobbled it down and then sat close by his feet to wash her face with a paw. He put his hands in the pockets of the overcoat and then realized he was hearing low voices behind him.

Seth stopped himself before he looked at the speakers—how many years had it been since he'd heard anyone speaking Farsi?

When he'd been a prisoner of war in Korea, he'd passed the weeks before his escape in learning scraps of other languages from fellow prisoners. After his return to the war zone, a high-ranking Marine officer realized Seth had a useful gift for absorbing languages.

"They must not be allowed to discover any of this information," an elderly-sounding voice said.

"Do you take me for a fool?" another, younger male voice answered irritably. "When do we next meet?"

1

"In two days, at this quiet spot again. No one here has the slightest interest in either of us; the man on the bench, the one who is near my age, is merely sitting with his cat."

Amused at being the focal point of the conversation, the retired Marine kept listening.

The other voice snickered. "But he is not just an old man. Do you not see him clearly? He is obviously one of their top operatives. He is surely a spy, set to catch us in the very act of plotting against his country."

"Do not be so sure of yourself," the first voice warned. "Like you, I assume he is harmless. But we cannot be so certain of anyone else we may meet."

A throat-clearing and spitting sound was the only answer, then he heard two sets of footsteps walking away from each other. He looked down at the cat.

"We've overheard something no one would ever expect us to understand, haven't we, Midnight?"

The cat looked up at him, her paw stopped in mid-wash, studying him. She concluded that he hadn't any more food to offer her, so she resumed her bath.

"I have to go home," he stood up abruptly. "See you." *And I'll be sure to be here when they come back*, he added silently. *Who knows what else I could hear?*

Two days later, he brought the cat a canned sausage for her midday meal. After this treat, she allowed him to pick her up and stroke her rough fur once or twice.

"You look like you could use a home yourself," he told her, as the cat jumped off his lap and sat underneath the park bench. The empty rent envelope crackled in his overcoat pocket as he leaned against the bench back.

"It's not like I live at the Ritz," he continued the one-sided conversation. "I bet I could sneak you in and you'd have a warm place to stay at night. It gets nasty out here when the rains start." He waited a while; the pale sunlight was trying to warm the air but not making much headway. A man strolled past him; mid-thirties perhaps, bearded, talking on a cell phone—in Farsi. He walked past the veteran and sat down two benches away from his. Seth sank back into his coat, hunching his shoulders so he looked withered and powerless—and listened.

'Chabibi'—*that means he's talking to a sweetheart,* he translated as he eavesdropped. *Nothing to that conversation, probably.* He shook his head slightly at his own suspicious thoughts. *Too many years in Special Services, that's my trouble. If I had stayed in the shadows, loaned out from the Corps, I'd probably have retired from the CIA. If I'd lived to retire, that is. No wonder they supposedly had such a great retirement package. Who lived long enough during the Cold War to get it? No, it was better I went my own way; I don't have to watch my back that much anymore.* He caught movement out of the corner of his eye and carefully turned his head just a fraction.

Another foreign-looking, older man with a white beard was approaching the bench where the younger one sat talking. He sat down and offered one of the two box lunches he carried to the other man, who shook his head and went on talking. The first man, who looked to be in his late sixties or early seventies, motioned to him to hang up, but he again shook his head 'no' and kept talking. Exasperated, the white-bearded man looked around, and saw the vet sitting in the weak sunlight. He stood up, walked over to him and said in heavily accented English, "You could perhaps use some lunch?" as he held out the rejected box.

"Yes, thank you," Seth said, and took it. The cat appeared from nowhere, wrapping her lean body around his ankles as he opened the box and looked inside. The foreign man was already walking back to the other bench.

"Thank you very much," he said, raising his voice slightly so it would carry to his benefactor.

"You are welcome," the foreigner said, seating himself beside the younger man and opening his own box lunch. "It would appear your little friend is dining also."

The vet nodded in return, and offered the cat a bit of the ham from the thick club sandwich the box contained.

What are Middle Eastern men doing with ham sandwiches, he wondered. *Aren't they forbidden to eat pork?* The cat nipped at his fingers, wanting more. Seth took a bite, then fed the cat another scrap. *Looks like the white-bearded man's lunch has a turkey sandwich, so only the man in his mid-thirties is ignoring the strict diet of their religion.*

Finally finished with his conversation, the younger man snapped shut his cell phone and dropped it into his expensive jacket pocket. He scowled at the other man, who was wiping mayonnaise off his fingers with a paper napkin.

"Why didn't you eat before you came, as I did?"

"Why haven't you discarded all personal ties, as we were ordered?" the other man countered.

They were speaking in Farsi again.

I have to be very careful, the veteran reminded himself. *If they ever realize I understand what they're saying, I could be a marked man.* He chewed the sandwich slowly.

"Never mind that," the younger man spoke condescendingly to the elder one. "We are to go for training soon."

"You have been told we will be pilots?"

"No, the Director hasn't selected the pilots just yet. But we will all be given any training he thinks we may need. We shall serve a glorious purpose in fulfilling his plan, whatever our roles."

The older of the two nodded. "I shall be most happy in Paradise. My bones hurt now many hours of the night. Since my wife is dead and my large family scattered, I have no purpose any more."

"And my purpose shall be to take as many infidels with me as I possibly can," the younger one smiled.

Seth felt chilled, and not from the weather. He gave the rest of the sandwich to Midnight, his appetite gone. But then his old training kicked in, and he pulled the top off the dish of pudding included in the box lunch. He had to hear as much as he possibly could; eating from the enemy's table, so to speak, would give him an excuse to continue sitting—and listening.

These two are plotting something, or are part of a plot. Is it trouble for us? He didn't know what they were talking about—but he'd learned to trust his instinct for danger when he was in the military. It brought him through the war. He'd be damned if he were going to ignore that same instinct now.

They stood up. "I shall have plane tickets for us Monday," the man in his thirties said.

"Do we meet before then?" The younger one shook his head 'no.'

Today's Wednesday, Seth thought. *Who do I know who might be interested in what's going on?* The two walked towards him. *I need to appear nearly senile,* he reminded himself, and raised a hand as they came up to him, making it tremble as if from extreme old age.

"You youngsters are good to an old man," he told them, and smiled crookedly. *Too bad I still have all my teeth. If I could drool a little it would help.*

The white-bearded man looked closely at him. "We are not that far apart in age, it would appear to me. But—are you homeless?"

5

Seth drew himself up as if insulted. "I am only temporarily without quarters," he lied. *What'll they do about my answer?*

Reaching into a pocket, the older Middle Eastern man drew out his wallet. He picked out a twenty-dollar bill and held it out to him. "Here. This will not secure you lodging, but you will have a good dinner. Perhaps you may provide a bit of fish for your cat."

The veteran thanked him profusely, and babbled at the cat. "Look, Midnight, look what that good man just gave me. You want some nice fish tonight?" He smacked his lips.

The younger man sneered. "Why give the old fool money?" he asked, speaking Farsi again.

"The Prophet said we are to give to the poor always. This country is a disgrace, the way it neglects its old. Surely that must be one good reason for whatever punishment the Director is devising," the other man replied. He switched back to English. "Come, we must return to the office," and nodded good-bye to Seth.

"Thank you again, sir," the vet told him. *Too bad I don't have a hat I could take off, like Oliver Twist, and appear more like a grateful servant,* he thought to himself. He bent down and picked up the black cat. "C'mon, Midnight, let's go choose where we want to eat dinner tonight." He walked away, slowly, as if old age prevented him from moving any faster.

When the two Middle Eastern men were completely out of sight, Seth quickly retraced his steps and then hurried towards his small apartment. *I'll call my old lieutenant: he'll know who'd be interested in this little piece of information, probably his nephew. Let's make this information-trading thing a family affair.*

He locked the door behind him, seated the cat and himself on the sofa and reached for the phone.

"Roy? How are things going?"

They talked for a while about family and the few friends they kept in touch with, then Seth said, "Listen, I could use a little help down here. You remember how we scrounged around for stuff for special staging, for the USO and so on—we needed favors, we gave favors. Yeah."

He grinned at the phone. Unless they were face-to-face, his fellow ex-Marine always stuck to that story. It was better that way. No one listening would be able to figure out what the hell they were talking about.

"Well, I just got a bill for two risers for that charity talent show. I don't know what's going on—all the stage stuff was supposed to be donated. I need some help with this. I don't have money to pay anyone. No, I don't want to go to work at your recycling plant to earn money. I like being on the fringes of show biz. I'm an old man; you should show me more respect. See, you move to New Jersey, you lose your manners."

After he hung up the phone, he turned up the volume on the TV a little and told the cat, "I'm gonna go buy you a litter box and some cat food with that money. Somehow using dirty money for soon-to-be dirty litter seems appropriate." He left his apartment and walked two blocks to the store, returning in less than a half-hour.

Just as he finished settling the cat in her new quarters, his phone rang. "That'll be Roy's nephew," he told Midnight. "Hello?"

"Seth? It's Mike. How're you doing?"

"I need you to check on a bill in Jersey," the vet said. "Can I just mail it to you, and you'll take care of it?"

"Sure. But wouldn't you like me to come and get you and drive you over to pay it yourself?"

"No, no—it's not that important. But you'll need to take the time to take care of it yourself. You'll have maybe a little argument with them about doing something—you know, adjusting it."

Mike had been a "spook" in his Air Force career; he'd made it so hot for himself he'd had to come home and go to work driving a dump truck, just so his trail would go cold. And he knew his Uncle Roy still spoke with respect about the crusty noncom he'd served with in Korea. Seth had led a rescue effort which had saved lives, Roy's among them. Mike didn't know all the details about Seth's capture and later escape. Most guys didn't escape the North Koreans. But when Mike questioned his Uncle Roy about the whole story, he just laughed and claimed the top brass had to give Seth a Bronze Star to get him to go home.

"Seth, you don't have to worry. I'll take it straight to their office, and we'll get it fixed."

After hanging up, Seth got some typing paper and an envelope. He wrote down as much of the foreigners' conversations as he could remember, and included details like the club sandwich with ham in it that he'd been given. Then, he tore a page out of the *Times* and carefully folded it over the handwritten papers so only newsprint would show through the envelope. He dropped the letter in the corner mailbox just as the street light came on.

Friday, Mike checked his mail and found the letter, opened the envelope, and discarded the piece of newsprint.

Somehow I didn't think he was sending me something from the Arts section. Why do I have the feeling this is gonna be trouble? he asked himself. He sat down and kicked his recliner into unfolding. He read the note several times, the wrinkles on his forehead making him look like a Basset hound. Then he reached for his phone.

"No, I—uh—just please tell the Colonel I hope he has a quick recovery," he told the woman on the other end of the line. She'd been cordial but firm about not disturbing her husband, just home from the hospital. "I'm sorry to have bothered you, Mrs. Daily. I didn't know about his emergency appendectomy last week."

Damn, he thought as he folded his cell phone closed. *Now who do I call?*

Mid-morning on Monday, Seth was teasing Midnight into swatting at a piece of yarn. On the other end of his park bench sat a youngish man with a gray-blonde crew cut, who lifted a paper bag to his mouth every few minutes, then slumped back half-asleep. The ex-Marine shook his head as the white-bearded, kinder Middle Eastern man, the one who'd given him the money a few days earlier, strode past.

"You're too young to be hitting that stuff," Seth said disgustedly to the crew-cut man drinking from the paper bag. He spoke loudly enough for the foreign man to overhear. "You got a future ahead of you, sonny. Why do you want to throw it away being a drunk?"

"Shut up, old man," the crew-cut man said, slurring his words. "You have no businessh sticking your nosh into my businessh."

Seth looked at the Middle Eastern man as he sat down, again, two benches away.

"What you gonna do?" he asked. "These kids, they don't listen."

"I have noticed your country has young wastrels among your citizens," the foreigner said, disapproval in his voice. "Perhaps he grew up too much in the lap of luxury to be able to manage his own way now."

"You may be right," the old man replied, and picked up his cat. He stroked her fur as Midnight settled onto his lap. He appeared deep in thought as the same foreign man in his mid-thirties walked up.

Then a man and woman holding hands hurried towards the two men. The woman dropped the man's hand and ran up to the older foreigner who stood up as he saw her, and hugged him, crying in English, "Uncle Rashid! I cannot believe it! I have not seen you for so long!"

He stood and returned the hug, smiling and soon openly wiping tears from his eyes.

"Maryam, how good to see you, my lovely jewel. Truly, you are a treasure of a niece. But who is this?" He turned to her companion.

"This is Abdulaziz Alomari," she said, and the two men shook hands. Then both Uncle Rashid and the thirty-something man studied the boyfriend just introduced. Seth noticed the elderly uncle didn't introduce the two younger men to each other.

"I saw you in Germany." The man who'd met the uncle before in the park was speaking Farsi to the woman's companion. Rashid almost flinched; put his arm around his niece's shoulders and drew her close to his side.

Alomari peered at the other man. "Were you also in Hamburg?" But before he could answer, Rashid broke into the beginning conversation by turning to his niece.

"My dear one, you are continuing with your college studies, I hope?"

"No, my uncle; I am too old for such things now. But congratulate me; we are to marry soon."

He hesitated, and then said firmly, "No, Maryam. I forbid it."

"But Uncle Rashid, I have been married before—it is not commonplace that a widow may marry again."

"I forbid it," and Rashid folded his arms—and his face—into hard lines. "Your father is not alive; the family into which you married is no longer alive. You are the

10

daughter of my sister, and so I must be your guardian. You may not marry this man. I do not know him nor his family."

Seth watched all of this with fascination; it was like a play. He'd been pretending to read a discarded newspaper while Mike slumped back against the park bench; mouth open in either a pretended drunken stupor or sleep. Mike's Farsi was sketchy; he'd told Seth that he could understand military terms but not much else. Seth, however, had been fluent in conversational Farsi, and the language was rapidly returning to his memory.

Alomari, the would-be fiancé, looked surprised and then defiant. He drew his eyebrows together and leaned towards Rashid: "We may not marry?"

"I forbid it," Rashid repeated, more forcefully this time.

Peering at his newspaper as if nearsighted but actually looking over the top of the page, Seth saw the niece's hand disappear into her Uncle Rashid's overcoat pocket for a minute. *What had she slipped into his pocket?*

"Come, my love," she said to Alomari. "We will go home and discuss this; then figure out what we must do." She moved away from her uncle's protection and took Alomari's hand.

But Alomari wouldn't allow Maryam to lead him away. He planted his feet. "We have been living together already. It does not matter whether you approve. We will be married."

Seth saw Rashid put his hands in his pockets and the faintest change of expression on his stern face.

"There will be no wedding. And there will be no more discussion." He turned his back on the couple as his niece, almost pleading now with Alomari, drew him away at last. The other two men sat down on their usual park bench.

11

The man in his mid-thirties laughed harshly, mockingly.

"Family quarrels. What silly stupidity, in these days of all days! But then, he was stupid in Germany too. He is not intelligent. I would never put him in a position of leadership, no matter how tiny the project." He drew a box cutter from a pocket and idly picked at a hangnail with the tip of it.

"That will be enough," Rashid answered. "Do you have the information?"

"We are to take the train to Lackawanna."

"We're not flying anywhere?" Rashid sounded disappointed.

"Not yet. We're to report to Salim Makhadi, and he'll know what we are to do next." He grinned suddenly, and beneath the man's black beard Seth saw the edges of an old, puckered scar. "But I did not come here all the way from Germany to be stored away like discarded clothing. I shall have my mission, a glorious mission, and I shall be known forever in the history books."

The other man shook his head. "Whatever way we serve, it will be in the most useful way."

"I am descended from caliphs and sultans. I bear a proud and honorable name. I shall have a mission which will make my name one the little American children shall fear until the end of their yowling days."

"I served in the diplomatic corps with your father," the older man said, and sighed. "I never understood his determination that utter destruction of our Christian neighbors was the only way our lives could return to peace."

The younger man stood and spat at the older one's feet. "My father often questioned your bravery," he mocked the other man, whose face turned gray at the insult.

Watching them without turning his head, Seth saw Rashid's hands clench into fists.

"Mahmud ibn Billah," he said through his gritted teeth. "You will give me the train ticket you have for me, and then we shall go our separate ways. I do not need to be insulted by a young jackal who thinks the Director will someday appoint him his second-in-command."

Ibn Billah stretched lazily and then smirked. "And why shouldn't he?" he taunted. "Have I not trained many recruits? Have I not been in South America and other disagreeable places, willingly and quietly, serving the Director in whatever capacity he asked? I deserve to be placed in a position of much more authority. In fact, the Director should be honored by my very presence."

Silently Rashid held out his hand, and ibn Billah slapped a train ticket into the palm.

"Goodbye, old ghost," he said. "You may have been useful at the United Nations, but you have outlived your usefulness now."

"May you never again know a night's peaceful rest," Rashid said quietly; he rose from the bench and walked away.

Ibn Billah watched him leave and laughed. "I would not want a peaceful night in Paradise," he said. "I shall spend my nights immersed in delights of which you have never dreamed." He turned and walked in the opposite direction.

Mike sat up and abruptly discarded his pretense of being drunk. "What was that all about?"

Seth was still watching the direction ibn Billah had taken. "Don't be too sober just yet," he cautioned. Mike looked at the old vet, then pulled the paper bag from his pocket.

Just as ibn Billah walked by them again, Mike said belligerently, "Quit trying to help yourself, shilly stupid old fool. Go buy your own bottle."

"I wasn't trying to take your liquor!" Seth protested. "Go somewhere else and sober up."

Ibn Billah looked carefully at both of them, apparently assuring himself they were of no importance, and kept walking, now traveling in the same direction Rashid had taken.

They waited for ten minutes before they spoke again. "How did you know he was going to come back this way a second time?" Mike demanded.

"He wanted to be sure we hadn't understood what they were saying," Seth said quietly. "Dear God, I wish your Colonel hadn't been out of commission."

"It's okay," Mike shrugged. "Emad and I can wing it if we have to—we've done it before. But so far I don't see or hear anything that we could take to someone who'd have any authority to trail these two or snoop into their actions."

Some blocks further up the street, Maryam was still having trouble with Alomari.

"Why must you listen to your aged uncle?" he whined. "We are in America now; you do not have to obey the old laws." Maryam practically dragged him along, her arm around his waist, ignoring looks from other people. He didn't need to know she'd carefully planned that meeting with her uncle.

"He is the head of my family now," she said quietly. "Quit fretting. Let him get used to the idea." She turned her face up to his and smiled as brilliantly as if she meant it. "After all, I could never go on living without you, could I? And you could not exist without me. We shall stay together, never fear."

14

Late that night she sat in the grimy kitchen of the cramped walk-up apartment they shared. Alomari snored heavily in the tiny bedroom; she'd given him enough liquor to first make him silly and then sleepy. Drunk, he'd leave her alone for the rest of the night. And as long as she praised his prowess the next morning, the fool kept believing she was in love with him.

I hope dear Uncle Rashid read my message on the inside of that gum wrapper. That way he'll know I'm not aligned with this jihad. But how have they snared Uncle Rashid? His heart can't be in this; he's never condoned violence. She worried, and slowly sipped a soda as the old memories emerged again.

The only thing that had kept her sane, kept her surviving the prison—the abuse, the rapes—had been her hatred of Saddam Hussein. The prison guards delighted in her grief over her husband's agonized death, and she had vowed revenge against the ones most responsible.

When she was abruptly released without explanation, that very night she had crept back into the prison and quietly cut the throat of one particular guard in the foul darkness.

But her own punishment continued after her release, for she found only more horror: her dearest sister in name, Rabiah Aslam, was long dead—stoned to death—and her brother-in-law Emad had vanished. She knew her husband Daud's other two brothers had died cruel deaths. Her former home in a luxurious part of the Baghdad suburbs was silent and empty. Her beloved parents-in-law had died of grief and anxiety, or so said the few neighbors who dared speak to her.

When a heavily-disguised member of *al-Qaeda* slipped close to her in a crowded marketplace one morning and asked in a whisper if she would be interested in a "vote against oppression," she had answered yes. Soon, amid a

15

fervent pretense of now completely belonging to *al-Qaeda*, she began planning. If only somehow, with the help of God, she could destroy Hussein by using *al-Qaeda's* weapons and training—that ought to be fitting justice.

Two days later, Seth was saddened by a brief article in the morning paper. An unidentified man's body, apparently of Middle Eastern descent, had been found under thick shrubbery in the same park where he and Midnight went each day. According to the reporter, police would only say that the body was that of an older man, possibly in his seventies, without any identification and yet with a train ticket to Lackawanna in an overcoat pocket. Cause of death was tentatively listed as homicide—the man's throat had been cut.

In April, Maryam began to wonder just what she'd gotten herself into—suddenly Alomari had money, lots of money, and no reasonable explanation as to why. He insisted they move to a luxurious apartment near the financial center of lower Manhattan. Its huge windows opened to a view of the New York skyline usually only seen in the movies.

Her "fiancé" began buying cameras and taking photos. He spent his days walking the streets around the World Trade Center complex of buildings and taking hundreds of photos each week. Alomari had a pair of powerful binoculars that he wore around his neck when he left the apartment on weekends, and a bulging file of maps of New York.

Maryam, of course, had to quit her job at a private school when Alomari insisted on moving, and now she trailed Alomari sometimes when he left, trying to figure out why he was so fascinated with the World Trade Center. Its buildings seemed to be the focus of all his information-gathering efforts, and her uneasiness grew after she recalled the bombing in 1993. She got a part-time job in a bank close to the WTC, and insisted Alomari walk with her each time she went to work. But she still couldn't persuade him to tell her what he was doing.

He went on three business trips—or so he said—without her, and then oddly, when summer arrived, he went to Florida for six weeks. When he returned, she challenged him, grabbing his suitcase out of his hands at the door to their apartment, pretending she thought he met another woman and had an affair during the time he was gone.

He laughed at her, while she continued the farce of beseeching him to tell her who the woman with whom he'd spent most of the summer was. Finally, after she'd plied him with enough bottles of beer, he became talkative.

"I've learned to fly!" he boasted. "I've been taking flying lessons—I am a pilot now!" She stared at him.

"You mean to tell me you haven't been with another woman?"

He leered at her. "I could certainly handle another woman. I am truly too much for one such as you, my pigeon. I could easily find many women, younger women who have more meat, more plumpness and who would swoon after I merely touched them—but no, I was not with a woman. Unless you count an airplane as a female." He giggled, started to tilt the beer bottle to his mouth again, and then slumped against the chair in which he sat. The bottle tipped in his hand, and he watched the beer pour out of the bottle and splash onto the thick carpeting, too drunk to correct his grasp.

Maryam hurried to the kitchen to get a wet dishtowel and blot up the beer. *What is he up to now? He's too stupid to figure out the TV schedule without my help; why was he taking flying lessons?*

He resumed his photography "'hobby'" and started going out alone after whispered phone conversations. She couldn't get him to walk with her to work anymore; he said he was too busy and the streets of New York were too hot in the August heat. Sometimes she would come home from work and find far too many dirty dishes in the sink for only his use. A small carton of box cutters turned up in his sock drawer, next to the ornate case which had held the heavy wristwatch to which he'd treated himself. The very brand name told her it would have cost her years of part-time paychecks at the bank.

The last week in August, he came home with an expensive briefcase which he kept by his side, locked at all times and watched over more carefully than he would have a small child. It had a gold Hand of Fatima dangling from the handle. She tried to coax him into telling her what it contained, but he set his jaw and refused to talk to her. She couldn't get at the briefcase to try and pick its locks, because Alomari was no longer sleeping in their apartment. When he grew tired and sleepy, he would call a cab and take the briefcase with him into the night. Where he spent his nights, she didn't know.

The first day of September came and Alomari announced he was traveling to Portland, Maine. She begged to go with him, knowing some plan had at last been set in motion, but he was adamant about her remaining in New York: "So you can see my glorious project and watch as my name is inscribed in the rolls of history."

The door closed behind him, and she still stood, wondering what she could do next. She had no friends in government agencies; didn't even know where the nearest FBI office was located.

What could I tell them, anyway? I'm suspicious there might be a plot against the United States, and that it might involve the World Trade Center?

She was no longer receiving any communications from *al-Qaeda*—hadn't since she'd contacted her Uncle Rashid, as a matter of fact—but she was watched by someone from that organization. Shadows were diligent in following her. That was one reason she continued to live with Alomari, even though she loathed him, hated it whenever he touched her. Anyone in the outside world she spoke to about her suspicions would think she was crazy.

Sometimes she wondered herself.

Twilight

Nine days later, the phone in the apartment rang just as she got home from her job at the bank.

It was Alomari, sober but strangely excited; his voice was tense and his words carefully chosen, almost as if he read from a script.

"The time is near. Watch the news tomorrow, my sweetling. Watch and let your breast swell with pride as I have my name inscribed in letters of fire." And he hung up the phone.

Maryam lay awake that night. She tried to pray, asking God for guidance as to what she should do, but her conscious mind was too agitated to think clearly, let alone still itself so she could listen for any answer. She fell asleep for an hour near dawn, but woke, gasping for air.

She wearily dressed and went to the windows of the apartment, opening them to let in any breeze. She wasn't supposed to work today, but she felt like she needed to go for a walk; anything was better than pacing the floor or watching for—what?

What terrible thing is about to happen as I watch without being able to help?

She drank a cup of coffee and tried again to call her Uncle Rashid, using the only number she had for him. The phone rang and rang. She imagined it finally annoying his neighbors and gently placed the handset back on the receiver. Maryam went to get her purse and stood at the windows again, scanning the sky for a few minutes? An hour? She never knew.

Because as she turned to start out the door, she caught a glimpse of a low-flying plane on the horizon. It hit the World Trade Center tower at 8:48 a.m. She threw up her coffee in the kitchen sink.

The horror of it made her stagger as she was drawn back to the windows again, just in time to see the second plane hit the next tower.

"God forgive me," she whispered. "I should have tried harder to find someone to warn." Whirling, she ran out of the apartment and to the elevator. Once in the street, she ran towards the World Trade Center, just as other people were doing.

Perhaps I can help get people out of the buildings, she thought. *Maybe take their hands and lead them away from the buildings after the fire fighters and police have guided them downstairs.*

She ran faster, listening to the odd sounds of the crowd around her. Most people had stopped running now; they were standing and staring as if their feet suddenly held them to the spot. She heard gasps and moans, then agonized sentences.

"They're leaping from the buildings!" one man said, waving his arms, tears streaming down his face. "They're getting out the only way they know, jumping before they burn to death!"

She ran past TV reporters, people carrying cameras, other people crying and collapsing on the sidewalk. She had a terrible pain in her ribs and side but she ignored it. She had to keep running.

She darted around a police blockade and ran into the auditorium. The strange noises: firefighters running, their booted feet making slapping sounds on the polished floors; people moaning or screaming while they pressed their fists against their mouths, the peculiar roar of fire out of control, sounded like the soundtrack from a horror movie. Several people were slowly picking their way across the mounds of debris, moving away from the stairwell. Two men appeared to be struggling, carrying someone else between them;

21

panting, they gasped encouragement to their burden and to each other as they staggered towards what she thought were the outside doors. It was hard to tell. There were no real reference points any more. She turned in a circle, wondering, searching–no one seemed to need the scant help she could offer. She hurried past the seats in the auditorium and suddenly turned, grabbing hold of one of the seat backs just in time to keep herself from falling into them. A shadow was scrabbling along in the gloom. To her disgust, it seemed to be searching among the clothes and pieces of suitcases; purses, shoes, jackets that were tangled amid the ruined seats.

"What are you doing?" she challenged the figure. "Leave those things alone, you carrion-picker!" She was mad—angrier suddenly than she had ever been in her life. She clenched her fists and ran towards the end of the aisle, trying to stop the looter. "Put those things down! Leave them for their families—it's all they have left of the people they loved!" Her voice rose into a shriek, and suddenly she felt the building itself shudder. She was close enough to the looter to hear him choking on the thick dust. He turned and growled obscenities at her.

She stopped suddenly and nearly fell, her feet sliding on the dust and trash beneath her. In the dim light, close to the looter's feet, she saw Alomari's briefcase.

That briefcase! Three seats away, the briefcase Alomari had guarded so fiercely was lying on its side; blackened, dented and small conical feet missing. She knew it was the same metal briefcase—she had studied it too many times, trying to figure a way to wrest it away from Alomari's grasp. The gold Hand of Fatima still dangled from the handle, and Alomari's extremely expensive watch lay beside it.

The building groaned again, and she looked up to see the ceiling rushing towards her. The looter grabbed both the expensive watch and the Hand of Fatima just as Maryam snatched the briefcase. She yanked at it with all her strength, and the tiny chain broke. She backed up a few steps and started running again, hoping in the sudden billows of choking black smoke that she was moving out of the building and not further into it. She reached an outside door finally; just as she sucked in one more gulp of somewhat breathable air and pushed her way out, the tower collapsed. She fell outside the doorframe, cutting her knees on broken glass and trying desperately to continue breathing. *I have to get this briefcase to someone who knows what to do about it!*

She counted to ten, then forced her body up off the shards of glass and onto the sidewalk, into the belly of a roiling monster of smoke and debris. Bricks and chunks of concrete struck her as she picked her way over piles of paper and trash. Her stomach heaved as she saw what looked like a hand, curled as if begging for help, but without a person attached to it. Slipping and sliding, she skirted the smoldering ruins and held her blouse up over her mouth and nose with one hand while she clung to the briefcase with the other.

Somehow she was up against another building, but in which direction it stood from the World Trade Center, Maryam had no idea. She drew her elbow along the walls which were still standing, finding her way out to the street and joining the other people who looked like gray cement statues staggering, falling, getting up at the urging of those with them and scrambling on. The sounds of car alarms and the eerie absence of the normal noises of a huge city set her shivering during her walk back to what had been home.

She found her way to the apartment and got inside just before the building was sealed off and everyone evacuated. Everything was under a layer of gray cement dust; so thick it had drifted already, obscenely tracing every

23

detail of whatever object lay underneath it. She got her car keys and left the apartment, taking nothing but her purse and the briefcase.

The parking garage was only three blocks away, but already it had been sealed off too. She joined the line of weary people heading for the ferryboats.

I'll get off the island and wait until I can retrieve my car. And then I'll take the briefcase—somewhere.

Maryam used her credit card to rent a shabby motel room somewhere in New Jersey, wherever the bus from the ferry area had dropped her off. The desk clerk hadn't questioned her or asked why she had no luggage other than the briefcase. He took one look at her dirty, bloody face and silently pushed the room register towards her. She signed her name, then went to her room and started the shower running.

Once under the steaming water, she let the tears come and cursed Alomari and all his associates with every vile, vicious imprecation she could manage. She cursed them all, their children's children, and the five generations after that, until she couldn't think any more. The soap stung in the scrapes and cuts from the flying glass and bricks which had struck her as she fought her way out of the hell that had been the tallest, proudest buildings in the world.

Three days later, her cuts starting to heal, Maryam was working double shifts every day at Ground Zero until near collapse, hauling buckets of debris, bringing masks to other volunteers, sinking down exhausted onto a stool behind a counter so she could hand out sandwiches and water as she rested.

She caught her breath as a man walked past the sandwich counter. He looked like her dearly loved brother-in-law, Emad Aslam! Could it be? She stopped herself before she called out.

He disappeared years ago; it couldn't be him. And if it is him—was he involved in this hideous, twisted vengeance upon the Americans too?

Her mind argued back and forth, getting nowhere.

Was that man Emad or not? Was he involved in the plot? She was relieved by another volunteer worker and she hurried outside, just in time to see the man who looked like Emad walk out of one of the water tents on Liberty Street and towards a huge dump truck on the edge of the driving area. He swung himself up into the driver's seat and started the engine. He was a volunteer too, then—her heart skipped a beat.

Surely he can't be involved in the plot! The man she'd known so many years so long ago, who believed in treating everyone fairly and decently, was still among the living and now helping people yet again. Tears ran down her face but she didn't feel them. Another volunteer came by and shook her arm gently.

"You're getting too tired," the other woman said softly. "Go home. Get some rest. You'll still be needed tomorrow."

"Where do the dump trucks go?"

"They're going to an abandoned Staten Island garbage dump. They're taking all the—debris—there so everything can be spread out and carefully searched."

Maryam strained her eyes to see past the still-rising smoke and read "Environmental Solutions" on the side of the truck.

Two days later, a small black car followed two dump trucks through the Holland Tunnel to Hoboken, passed the trucks as they turned into the gate of "Environmental Solutions," and continued on its way.

Chapter One

They didn't find the briefcase until they got back to New Jersey. It had been another long, disheartening day—fourteen hours long, to be specific.

"Crane," Mike gestured "up" with his head.

"OK," Emad called. Together they lumbered the two big dump trucks out of the way. Mike watched as the huge yellow crane moved horizontally over them to lift a sixty-ton contoured concrete chunk that had been part of the World Trade Center, and deposit it to the side. In the humid heat of a New York late September, the smell and smoke of the still-smoldering fires was acrid, gagging. Many of the people at the site wore white respirator masks, so the area looked like an improbable hospital ward. Mike could feel pulverized concrete dust clinging to his eyelashes and the hairs inside his nose. "Let's take a break," he told Emad over the walkie-talkie, and they pulled the dumps further to the side and parked them.

Climbing down out of the cab, Mike felt eighty years old. And helpless. And still madder than hell. Only a week after the World Trade Center had crumbled, he'd known they weren't going to find any survivors. Now it was barely two weeks, and the steelworkers, other construction workers and big cats were here to clear away the tons of debris—and avoid thinking about the thousands of people who literally were dust.

They walked to one of the tents on Liberty Street to get bottles of cold water. Mike started to wipe his face on his shirtsleeve, and then realized that wasn't a good idea. His sleeve was as dirty as his face. All the workers had been warned not to rub their eyes and risk the fine dust damaging their vision, but to go to a first aid or eyewash tent.

"I'll be right back," he told Emad. He walked past a man who'd taken off his facemask and poured a bottle of cold water over his head. The water washed enough of the man's face clean to show an ugly, puckered scar running from the outside corner of his left eye diagonally across his face to his chin.

He looks like an extra in some of those old WWII movies, Mike thought. *The Third Reich and their dueling scars. Brother.*

Emad sipped at his water, and then held some in his mouth for a moment, savoring its pure sweetness. He, too, noticed the other worker, a firefighter judging by his shirt, as he started to put his facemask back on.

"Don't try to reuse that," he told the younger man. "They've got plenty in the fourth tent, that way." He pointed. "Throw that one out."

The firefighter studied him for a minute, then nodded, once. "Gracias," he said; he threw the old mask in a wastebasket and walked out of the tent, carrying a white pail with tools in it.

Mike rejoined Emad. "Wanna take some sandwiches back to our trucks?"

"Good idea."

Break over, they started their trucks and moved back into position. Hours went by. Machines shuffled debris from the heaps and mounds of wreckage to each truck, pausing only when sharp-eyed workers spotted a possible bit of humanity in the grisly waste.

"This is a democratic worksite," Emad's voice crackled over the walkie-talkie as they rolled out of the area. "Everybody has a choice of getting killed, from cave-ins, death stink, this goddam concrete-like talcum that chokes you."

27

"Jesus!" Mike veered sharply to the left. He'd skinned the side of the dump truck on a jagged piece of rebar that stuck out horizontally from a former footing.

"See, you're weaving. I think the noxious fumes got to you. Or maybe you like fumes, like sniffing benzene."

"I think the fumes have gotten to you. You're developing a weird sense of humor." Mike shifted gears, pulled up and stopped so other workers could hose off the sides and tires of the dump. The quick wash kept most of the dust and dirt confined to the site.

"Enough for now," Emad said. "Twelve hours again; we're getting punchy."

"I hate to leave."

"Look," Emad pointed to the rows of other trucks waiting to get in to start their grim work. "It's early in their day. Let them get a chance to help."

"OK," Mike nodded, turned off the walkie-talkie and eased his dump over in front of Emad's to lead the way one more time. They had kept doggedly on, like everyone else during these weeks of 12-hour days. It took an hour to get to the repository, an abandoned Staten Island garbage dump for everything hauled from the disaster site. Then another hour to Hoboken, to Uncle Roy's recycling yard. They slept, got up, went back to the pit. Days blended in Mike's mind, along with the numbness of not finding survivors: they needed just to work, to do what they knew, to try to do something.

They lumbered through the Holland Tunnel and north on the side road toward Hoboken, past a line of one-story commercial buildings strung like beads—a car wash, a body shop, a thrift shop, a place that repaired vacuums. Then the neighborhood changed into blocks of older two-story wood duplexes, small front lawns and a hydrangea bush near each front door, as they approached the yard.

"Beer?" Emad asked as he finished washing out his truck.

"Bed," Mike answered. "I'm getting to be an old man. I'm going home as soon as I finish here. Grab another sandwich, then six beautiful hours—" He leaned in to get his car keys out of the glove box.

"What the hell!" Something was on the floor of the dump truck, where a passenger's feet would rest. He pulled it out of the semi-darkness and when he realized it was a damaged, possibly booby-trapped briefcase, threw it some feet away from Emad and himself. They both ducked behind the truck fender as the briefcase hit the dirt, then opened with a loud snap, revealing tissue-thin pages closely covered with writing.

They walked over to it.

"Arabic," Emad said softly. "Interesting, my friend."

Chapter Two

Air Force Special Ops and the CIA had put Mike and Emad together as a targeting team. Mike Braun was a first lieutenant—Emad Aslam, an Iraqi who'd been recruited by the CIA several years before the Gulf War. He'd worked undercover, sometimes spying, sometimes as a go-between for various factions. But always his main purpose had been to topple Saddam Hussein.

They'd been in danger many times, risking death by friendly fire, hoping the bombs overhead would hit their targets exactly and not wander into their vicinity. And they'd worked well together, becoming friends as they completed assignments.

When the Gulf War ended it was unsafe for Emad to be anywhere in the Middle East. So Mike suggested a "working vacation."

"I got an uncle owns a little trucking firm in New Jersey. He hauls gravel, crushed rock, construction debris, that sort of thing. I'm getting out of Special Ops and going to work for him. Why don't you come along?"

The yard had formerly been called a dump, but two years ago Mike's uncle, Roy Braun, had changed its sign outside to "Environmental Solutions" and put up a big recycling circle of three arrows.

"How the hell did that get here?" Mike demanded, pointing at the mutilated briefcase.

"It was put in your truck somehow," Emad responded. He lifted the briefcase up out of the dirt and set it on a recycling bin. His long thin fingers shifted from one page to another.

He looks, Mike reflected, *as much the opposite of the caricature of stubble-faced Arab as you can imagine.* He looked like what he was: the last of a long line of Aramaic scholars, somehow turned truck driver.

Now his expression was saturnine, concentrating, one forefinger parting his lips in a slight smile; aquiline nose, dark eyes burning under black bushy brows, which contrasted with his white hair—parted, full, vigorous. He had a gray beard, which did not diminish his air of assurance. It was a face that caused women to flick their eyes, looking at him in short darts, almost as if they were afraid of him realizing their interest.

In his face one could read the history of another world—a world of thick, rolled texts on goat hide, high walls, and men who wrote complex poetic lines with ink-stained fingers. It was a world from which Saddam Hussein had long felt excluded. That exclusion was reason enough for the Republican Guard to arrest Emad's three younger brothers and for Hussein to put Emad on his personal hit list. During all the years of their friendship, about the only thing Mike knew was that Emad's brothers had died in Section 7 of Hussein's torture chambers. He understood the pay back Emad sought—scholar or not, he'd lost his entire family to a sadistic killer.

Now this development. Mike knew in his gut that this was going to mean another mission for them—their old jobs would haunt them the rest of their lives.

Two weeks earlier, before the dust cleared after Tower One collapsed, Uncle Roy called his nephew Mike and Emad to his office. Pointing through the window, across the Hudson, he said, "That dust cloud is where you guys are gonna spend the next months, or year, or however long it takes. I've already called the Port Authority and volunteered your services in whatever capacity they need. They want you there at noon tomorrow. You'll be hauling debris to a site on Staten Island; they'll fill you in on the details when you get there. We start small. Clear one little area." He swallowed hard.

Roy Braun had been through Korea, lost his best friend there—but this was worse than any war. He kept his face still. The first time Emad saw Roy he'd realized how much Mike looked like his uncle. Mike's face was starting on the same basset-hound folds as his uncle's; they were both built like bulls and had close-cropped Nordic blond hair going gray on the sides, above ears that stuck out.

"And guys—if you want to get out of the rigs and carry buckets instead, that's OK by me. Wear your photo IDs around your necks; they're not letting anyone in without one. Whatever you can do that'll help, you got my backing. They need everyone they can get to help find people and get them outta there." His usually calm face tightened. "We'll get everybody out that's still alive. And then the bastards that did this are gonna pay."

It was a long speech for Roy, and Mike knew from that just how deeply his uncle's feelings ran. He seldom revealed much of what he thought, but liked to recount his experiences. During the post-Gulf War years, they'd swapped a lot of war stories over a beer with the still crew-cut ex-Marine.

Now this situation. The briefcase was about a foot and a half by two feet, aluminum, with a handle, broken locks, hinges and pieces of what once were small conical feet. It looked expensive and was well constructed, except for badly dented corners. The papers inside were onionskin, charred or browned at their edges, some fused together from the horrific heat. Emad picked up one of the charred pieces of paper and held it toward the spotlight under which they'd been scrubbing out the dump trailer. He sucked air in through his teeth and swore under his breath.

"Someone planted this on your truck! There are three billion pounds of debris pulled out of this site, plus two giant planes and parts of people scattered everywhere. How does this particular briefcase end up with us?"

"Why would someone plant it?"

"I don't know. But I do know these pages need translating. They could lead us to some interesting people."

"You're taking some jump to that conclusion—" Mike began.

"There isn't much in that site anybody can recognize. No furniture, just little things from desk drawers, handbags. I saw stamps, marketing lists. The paper items did better than the people. I saw cell phones, loose change. And earrings. A worker told me in Staten Island that so far they found 119 earrings. Earrings for no ears—what irony. The jewelry survived. And these papers look a lot like pages the media described, which were found in the rental car at Logan Airport."

Mike sighed. "How did I know you were going to say that? C'mon. We'll go to the office, make copies of whatever's legible. And then we'll call our old bosses."

It took until 2 a.m. to carefully lift the papers free from the warped carcass of the briefcase and copy each page that could be salvaged.

"I can't believe this much stuff stayed intact," Mike said. "Somebody at the site was saying each floor was crushed down to a foot or so in depth. Tower Two fell at about 200 miles an hour."

Emad looked at the stack of copies. "I think translating this is going to give me nightmares."

Mike flipped open his cell phone. "Didn't think I'd ever call this number again." He looked at Emad. "They're gonna tell us we're too old to do the fighting this time. But are you willing to do everything else?"

Emad nodded. "Bet on it. I'll call the Company after you check in with the brass."

Chapter Three

A day later, in stifling heat reflecting off tan walls of a cubbyhole office in Langley, Virginia, Colonel William Daily looked at the smashed briefcase and the neat pile of copies next to it on the table.

Lieutenant Manuel Sierra, Daily's aide, produced an exaggerated wrinkling of his nose.

"Amazing what garbage men can find these days. We should add a new section to training."

"Napoleon," Mike ambled beside him, to loom over the lieutenant. "So, they haven't got rid of you yet? We thought we'd never see you again."

Sierra frowned. He stood 5 foot 7 in his paratrooper boots, which had inch-and-a-half heels. Mike, without boots or shoes, stood 6 foot 2.

Sierra walked around to the other side of Daily's desk. "Maybe you didn't notice, but that's why you're pushing around garbage bins. You've been dumped too. I don't know what all of this is—" he waved a delicate hand at the copies. "But for sure it's part of some bizarre calculation to get you two back in."

"Enough!" Daily barked. "Sit down, men. You said some of the pages crumbled after you copied them," he turned to Mike. The Colonel's forearms rested on top of his desk, the skin striated with age, glasses perched low on a waxy nose. But behind his glasses the eyes were gray, commanding—not the eyes of a man nearing retirement.

"That sounds convenient," Sierra's grin was mirthless. "How did you manage that, drop them in gasoline?"

"That's why we copied them, sir. We realized they were extremely fragile." Mike was acutely aware of Daily's discomfort at Sierra's needling remarks.

"I'm adding some more people to this right away. Emad, keep working on your translations. We're going to have to coordinate this through several offices, and I don't want time or manpower wasted. You've got a set to work with?"

"Of course they do," Sierra nodded his head. "Like I said, *convenient*."

"Get out of here, Manuel," Daily shook his head. "Mike and Emad were the best operatives I've ever seen. You could learn something if you lost that attitude."

Sierra regarded him evenly. He shrugged, rose to full military bearing and left. His parting glare showed he wasn't to be placated with anything Mike and Emad had cooked up.

"How the hell did you get stuck with Sierra?" Mike asked after the office door closed.

"It seems over the years I've made a few enemies in the Agency. Plus his flyboy uncle, his mother's brother, is a general. Sierra is their pipeline into my office."

"Our prints are on everything too, Colonel," Emad reminded him.

"I'm sure they're still on file somewhere, along with your clearances," the Colonel replied dryly. "For now, I want both of you to go back to your shifts at Ground Zero. Act as normal as possible. Keep your eyes peeled but stick to your routine. I'll get back to you."

Mike and Emad stood and walked to the door.

"You still don't know how that particular piece of debris ended up in your truck," Colonel Daily said. It was a statement, not a question.

"No, sir," Mike answered. "I wish we did." He closed the office door behind them.

"He looks older," Emad said softly as they left the dimly lit building for the bright sunlight. "And what was all that crap with Sierra?"

"Sierra has other problems beyond being lazy. He figured he was a cinch to be the Company's Hispanic poster boy, but he got derailed. So now he's an aide, just putting in his hours. But he hasn't forgotten. He wanted to be the next James Bond."

Emad shook his head. "He's not much help to the Colonel. And now we're up against some of the same people we thought we'd dealt with in the Gulf. Fighting the same scum over and over ages you."

"That's what's aged the Colonel," Mike replied.

Seven days and matching 12-hour plus shifts later, Mike and Emad drove their big dump trucks through the gates of the yard at Environmental Solutions. They again washed out both trailers, hosed off the tractors one last time, and then headed for their cars.

"What's Uncle Roy still doing here?" Mike asked, as they saw lights on in the second story office.

Emad headed for the stairs. "Let's find out."

A man in a New Jersey Department of Transportation uniform was sitting across from Roy as they entered the neat office. Roy stood, came from behind his desk, grinning briefly as both truckers looked surprised at the sight of Colonel Daily posing as a DOT officer. The ex-Marine moved toward the window as the Colonel changed places with him.

Roy glanced through the window, then opened the door. "You guys talk to the nice man from DOT and get that paperwork done tonight. Leave it on my desk and I'll finish it in the morning." He nodded and left the office, jingling the change in his right pants pocket as he limped towards his car. Emad locked the door behind him.

"Your uncle is one helluva Marine," Colonel Daily said. "Makes me believe all those recruiting posters." He looked at his watch. "I'll make this as short as possible. You guys are going to be OTR truckers, driving team in a rig with a special sleeper on it. We've coded this 'Operation Storm Watch'—you're going to be weather trackers." He smiled as Mike and Emad looked at each other, startled. "What, you thought you were going to get off easy because you're too old for Special Ops anymore?"

Emad looked steadily at the officer. "A man is never too old to repay a blood debt."

"True. But—you are too old." They started to protest. Colonel Daily waved them quiet. "Too old to lead the charge. I reviewed your files," he nodded at Mike. "You're coming up on 50. Your file, on the other hand," he said as he swiveled his chair to Emad, "has a lot of interesting blanks—and one of them is precisely how old you are. But you're not too old to be point men for the operation, and that's what you'll be doing. We're going to try to get you five or six hand-picked people to actually be on the front lines." He paused, took a deep breath.

"Your directive is simple: find and disrupt any terrorist activities or plans as you've seen them outlined in the papers from that briefcase. We're assuming some of those plans are red herrings, some are in the first stages, some are at an instigation point. Of course, we don't know which are which. That's your job. We're reactivating your code names from the Gulf: Mike, you're 'Striker' again; Emad, 'Lightning.' These will be your CB handles while you're driving as well."

He cleared his throat. "You'll take the new rig we're outfitting for you wherever you need to, under cover of doing weather research for Environmental Solutions. You'll operate under DOT rules and regulations—including HazMat, if needed—in all 48 contiguous states, Canada and Mexico. Your truck will be customized with the latest in communications and computer equipment. We'll have a tag on you at all times via satellite. Don't try to do everything yourselves. Just be yourselves—ordinary, unshaven, mangy truckers."

"Thanks a lot, Colonel," Mike said. "You know, not all truckers drag their knuckles on the ground as they walk."

"One of the team members will be Lieutenant Sierra."

"Jesus!" Mike put his hands on the desk and leaned towards the Colonel. "We're stuck with little Napoleon?"

"He went around me," Colonel Daily said, "and the word came down this morning to put him on the team. He picked up on information about the money for the operation and apparently he figures it may be something major."

"You mean he figures it's a way for him to leapfrog over everyone to *be* a major," Mike said. "Maybe we can lose him somewhere in the middle of the country."

"How about the Grand Canyon?" Emad offered.

The older officer ignored their comments. "It's going to take another two weeks for your truck to be finished. We want you phased out of working at Ground Zero and replaced with two other operatives. They need to be in place in case something else interesting but unexplainable turns up at the World Trade Center site. You'll be dispatched by my office through the Qualcomm system aboard your truck. The President has asked for a new Cabinet position to be created. When that happens, you'll report only to me, or the new Cabinet Secretary, or to the Commander-in-Chief himself."

He paused. "Actually, I'm glad to have you both back in business. I meant what I said when I told Sierra you were the best I'd ever seen. You'll report to Quantico in two days, to be trained and given whatever updates we can find. More details later. Good night."

He stood, picked up a leather folder, checked the outside area from the window and unlocked the door. Opening it, Colonel Daily said, "It looks like your papers are all in order. See you in the inspection bay someday." He went down the stairs.

Mike and Emad waited until the Colonel left before they went out the door, watching carefully in the meantime to see if there were any unwanted guests hanging around the yard.

"So now what?" Emad asked, once they were at their cars, unlocking doors.

"We get to skip showers and watch our beards grow," Mike responded. "Oh, yeah, and we better get some calluses on our knuckles."

Behind an old parts-only dump truck squatted a figure dressed in black clothing. After the sounds of the two cars leaving died away, it rose and cautiously slipped through shadows to the stairs. It went up the stairs, took a moment to pick the lock and faded through the doorway.

Chapter Four

Karem left the small house, his eyes squinting in the glare of the sun. He was slight in build, and the fragility of his skeleton suggested his other known name, "The Spider." He had darting eyes and when it was necessary to punish someone, they would brighten and his lips would part over his prominent teeth.

He'd never known the orange groves and fig trees or the stone house they had owned or that his father wept for until his death. Karem had grown up in the Palestinian refugee camp called Shatilla, a camp where the stink of urine- and water-soaked carpet pervaded the tents. Behind those tents were mounds of discarded clothes contributed by a charity, then picked through by the refugees and left. The shoes on the pile were curled by the water that was hosed through the camp each evening.

His only schooling had been in a *Quran* school, which taught him how silly it was to treasure things. Americans treasured things: their fast cars, their fancy offices and huge houses, their money—even their government had to start an exercise program in the schools because their children were so lazy and fat.

He surveyed his operation as he walked, saw how well things were going.

It had been five years of hard work to establish his simple *jojoba* farm here in the middle of the desert near Mecca. It made the perfect front for *al-Qaeda,* and soon would accomplish its original purpose, *inshallah.* The wide valley provided an excellent base for surveillance, and soon, very soon, would strike the whore Americans and their Israeli lapdogs exactly when they had the illusion they were once again safe from violence.

Abdul Salam had just given his weekly report in his nasal whine and shown Karem his logbook detailing plane movements at the small airport next door to the *jojoba* farm. The man observed accurately during his work as a laborer at the airport. The one time he had proven inaccurate, failing to log every hour during one workday the previous month, Karem had used a braided leather dog harness to beat him to his knees, and to teach him teamwork and cooperation. At the farm, they said Karem had a violent temper, but he rejected such claims.

"I don't lose my temper," he would begin his usual recitation of denial. "We have had from our parents, generation by generation, an indication of how we must fight. We cannot allow anyone to be soft." He was a top lieutenant in his organization. Those who obeyed him said that whenever Karem screamed, he was always right. The Director confirmed this. So his righteousness—and abuse—continued.

He entered the back door of the main office, which led into the "storeroom." It was nearly totally dark inside, the windows covered by plywood. One bare light bulb dangled from the ceiling. A desk stood in the corner, a computer stored behind its doors; the phone messages, faxes and letters kept safely out of sight. A steep stairway had been anchored into a corner of the room for access to the roof, so they could watch who was coming. *Good, I hear the sentinel's footsteps. Our true purpose, to put balm on the mortal wounds of my people, is still shielded from the cursed mongrels.* He looked at his clerk.

"What's the schedule this week?" he asked.

"We have seven truckloads arriving and we are shipping out seventeen loads of our *jojoba* products to cosmetic firms." Muhammad stood uneasily, hurriedly kicking a wooden stool away from the desk. It was not a good idea to be caught sitting when Karem came in.

"We will be leaving this place soon," Karem hooked the stool with his foot and sat on it.

41

"Where will we go?" Muhammad was an adolescent who had been at the farm since he was thirteen. "Orders come here, we ship more and yet more each day—"

"The *Quran* teaches us that what is certain is change," Karem shrugged. "This place will be gone. There will be other places. You will be called to better service."

"But—"

Karem sighed. He was capable of being comforting and informal when it made it easier to manage or control a man. And this one was still just a boy. "You will receive exact instructions and you will do well." He smiled. "Or have you become in truth a farmer?"

"Of course not," Muhammad straightened. "I am a soldier."

Karem nodded. He had heard it all before. *Allah will determine who survives and who doesn't.* This young man was of no special value; but he could be of special use.

When life is as least as unbearable with a gun as without, when the thought of his children and his children's children, all with nothing, comes into a man's head, then he curses and reaches for a bomb. And that this Muhammad will be anonymous, that he will kill with little effort and almost no chance of exposure, that he will die serenely shall certainly drive his victims crazy. They will not even know which group sends him or why, until they get a phone call claiming responsibility.

He brought his thoughts back to the conversation. "Good. It is not something I tell you to do or not to do, then. It is something in our blood, which springs from the land Israel has stolen from us, the land the American oil leeches invaded. Continue your report."

Still standing at attention, Muhammad said, "We are expecting to have our last loads of aircraft parts by the next full moon."

"Ah, that is good." Karem licked his lips as he thought. The beard below his lips was thick and black, befitting a man of only 32 years.

If Allah will have me, I shall not see another birthday upon this world. I will indeed join my brothers in Paradise—after taking as many infidels to death as I can. "What else do we have to gather?"

Muhammad's eyes were bright; he'd been watching his commander, knowing the information he'd recite would be greeted with praise. "We need not gather any more supplies. Over the last years, we have been diligent. And now we have one hundred tons of ammonia nitrate, five hundred cylinders of propane, and almost three thousand gallons of plane fuel." He waited.

"Very good, Muhammad," Karem replied gravely. "And the detonators?"

"We will have the remaining components for the detonators also in one week. Then Ali says he will have them put together in only three weeks."

Karem clapped his hands. "When we have everything assembled and we have heard from the Director, then will we celebrate, my young Muhammad."

"Shall we invite the local people?"

Karem curled his upper lip. "Even those simpletons might become curious. Are you sure they suspect nothing? What of the airport?"

"The airport is surrounded by our field of alfalfa, nothing more. It will be mowed the afternoon prior to that evening's launch of the greatest small aircraft strike the world has ever seen! The noise of the mowers will prevent any ears from hearing the planes being removed from the hangars and their engines warmed up. And so may Allah mow our enemies down."

"And what were you saying of the *jojoba?*" Karem teased.

43

"We ship more every day. One buyer said there is to be a special feature in their department stores called 'Perfumes of Araby.' Their women shop in such places unaccompanied by a man." Muhammad was shocked at such behavior.

"Truly, their harlots cannot seem to satisfy their desires for our oils and unguents," Karem said.

Muhammad smiled. "Then they paint their faces with their own destruction."

Karem left the dark hole of an office for the intense sunlight once again. *What a young fool he indeed is,* he thought. *He has no idea he will not survive the next mission. Allah be praised, I was never so witless as this young cub. Truly it is a desecration to the Prophet for this one to bear his holy name.*

Chapter Five

The pace at Quantico was fast and furious. Mike and Emad spent their days learning just enough weather forecasting and monitoring to pose as part of a weather crew. They also trained using the newest technological surveillance gear. Nights were spent reading and studying manuals, trying to get up to speed on everything thrown at them.

"Jesus," Mike said, "I didn't realize being out of the loop for these past years would make everything so hard. I know I'm not used to all the gadgets and gizmos we've seen so far—not in ten short days! What we could've done during the Gulf War with a laser that you point—and then *listen* with it."

Emad looked up from the thick manual he was studying. "Just think about Hussein's scientists working for all these years too. They've probably supplied *al-Qaeda* with as many bells and whistles as we have. We have to figure out how to be one step ahead of the terrorists while remaining stealthily behind them—or so they think."

"Yeah, you're right," Mike agreed. "So I'll believe I'm smarter too, not just older. We'll stop those bastards somehow."

Emad stood, stretched, turned off the desk lamp and headed for his bedroom. "Bet on it," he said over his shoulder.

Mike chuckled. "Remember, old age and guile are supposed to beat out youth and energy every time."

The following morning was spent learning how to calibrate a Doppler radar unit.

"Life was simpler when we watched how the birds and other creatures behaved to know what the weather was going to do," Emad commented, as he and Mike walked towards the base cafeteria for lunch.

"What, you could tell it was going to rain when your camel spit in your eye?" Mike kidded him.

"I'm not going to dignify that with an answer, you diesel donkey," Emad replied. His grin disappeared into his beard as a very large shadow engulfed them from behind. They stopped walking.

As they turned, both their jaws dropped when they saw nothing but blue plaid.

Then they heard a thundering boom of a voice: "You guys Emad and Mike?"

Mike began to move his eyes skyward, tracking the voice, and when he finally met the gaze of the voice's owner, his neck was craned at almost ninety degrees. He swallowed with some difficulty and asked, "Friend or foe?"

Emad cut in: "If he says 'foe,' I will surely outrun you, Mike."

Thunder Voice chuckled, then said, "Just another trucker like you two. I'm Kenneth Williams, but everyone calls me 'Dino.'"

Mike was instantly on his guard. *The pose that we're just truckers is on a "need to know" basis. Who is this guy?*

"Well, Dino, state your business."

Just then, Lieutenant Sierra came from behind Dino, sneering as usual. "You two garbage haulers have just met a *real* trucker."

Mike gritted his teeth. "Napoleon." He turned back to Dino. "If he's your Crackerjacks prize, you ought to demand your money back."

Sierra narrowed his eyes but continued. "Master Sergeant Williams is the newest member of Operation Storm Watch. He's been driving trucks since 1995. And he's a small arms expert."

46

Emad had been studying Dino further. "Small arms? Never. This man could pick up a cannon and use it like a cork gun."

Dino grinned, the gap between his front teeth showing for a minute. Then he clipped Sierra gently on the shoulder with a fist the size of a hubcap. The slightly built lieutenant staggered, but kept his footing.

"I'm gonna enjoy workin' with these guys, Lieutenant. Let's go get somethin' to eat an' swap truckin' stories."

They all went through the serving line and then sat down at a large table against a side wall.

"So how long ya'll been truckin'?" Dino asked, as he started on a platter of fried chicken.

"About ten years," Mike answered, absently. *Why is Sierra at Quantico,* he wondered. *God help us if he's going out on any missions.*

"Just got my CDL," Sierra interrupted the fragmented conversation. "Piece of cake. You Special Ops prima donnas always try to make something easy look hard."

Just wait until I'm on the road, in my own rig, doing the spy thing. I'll show every one of you, in or out of your little stuffed uniforms. You shouldn't have looked down your gringo *noses at me all these years.*

Emad looked up from his plate at the start of Sierra's bragging. "It isn't whether something appears easy or hard, my young lieutenant. It's how your training and talent deal with it. 'A calf thinks God is a cow,' according to Rumi." He returned to eating while reading a small book cradled in his hand.

Sierra started cutting his steak in chunks and cramming them into his mouth. "I can handle a lot more things than you think, Mr. Arab Scholar." He chewed.

47

You're going to have a big change of attitude one of these days. One of these days you'll be thanking Allah that I was around to rescue your sun-dried hide.

Emad left the table to get some more grapes and an apple. Sierra grabbed the book Emad had been reading and started flipping through it. "What is this crap?"

"Probably another philosophy book. Put it back, Sierra. You can't read Aramaic," Mike told him.

Sierra had found a faded snapshot glued inside the back cover. "Who's the babe?"

Emad's long fingers withdrew the book from Sierra's grasp. "She was my wife."

The rest of the men at the table looked at Emad, surprised. Even Mike hadn't known Emad had ever married.

"Rabiah was considered quite radical in our group. She believed women in Iraq should have the same rights and privileges as the men. I cautioned her to be more careful, to speak less openly—but I also thought my position as a newly tenured professor would shield her." None of the other men stirred. Even Sierra was silent.

"I had gone to a conference in Cairo on ancient languages. During my absence, Rabiah was falsely accused of adultery and arrested by the Republican Guard. Instead of imprisoning her, however, they took her to a remote village and told the *imam* of what crime she was accused. Upon his orders, the villagers stoned her." Emad glanced at the photo and then slipped the book into his shirt pocket. "We had no children."

Mike tried to swallow the lump in his throat. In all the years he'd known Emad, he still had never heard all the horrors his friend had suffered.

Dino stood, nodded at Emad to ease some of the tension around the table, and picked up his platter now filled with bones. "I'm goin' after some more of that chicken. Anybody need somethin'? Carton of milk?" He looked at Sierra, who nearly choked on his coffee and then banged his cup down on the table.

Mike wouldn't let a grin slide across his face. "No, we're good, I think." He watched the huge man amble across to the line again. "Bet he played college football."

"Debating team," Emad said.

Sierra snorted. "Blacks aren't on debating teams."

Now Mike's eyes narrowed. "You know, Napoleon, that's one thing I've never liked about you. You're not only bigoted, but you fold everyone into stereotypes."

Dino returned with his second platter of chicken and three cartons of milk in one big hand. He sat back down, opened a carton and drank it in two swallows. "I bet, Lieutenant Sierra, if you'd drunk your milk and eaten your vegetables like your Mama told you to, you might've grown up to be quart-size instead of pint-size." Even with his voice deliberately quieted, Dino's words caused several people eating at another table to smile.

From under his eyebrows, Emad saw Sierra's hand tighten on his steak knife.

"Sergeant Major Williams, you'd do well to remember I am your superior officer. I outrank you," Sierra glared.

"Not exactly," Dino said, mildly. "I'm retired military. I'm just a trucker from Texas now. Don't have a rank."

"But you're about 50-gallon drum size, I think." Colonel Daily was suddenly standing behind Dino, his left hand on the big man's shoulder, his right hand holding a tray. "Move over, Lieutenant."

The Colonel sat down, nodding his thanks as Mike got up and took the emptied tray to a stand nearby. Colonel Daily spoke softly, even though the area should be secure.

49

"You men need to know that as of now, Mr. Williams is correct. None of us is officially military, including me and my staff. We're on loan, on 24-hour call to the Office of Homeland Security. It's already operational, even if CNN hasn't announced it. Information you gather comes to me, but Tom Ridge is our boss. We get orders from him, and we report directly back to him or to the President. No one else."

The table was quiet as each man ate.

Mike stood up after he'd finished. "Dessert for me. Anybody else?"

Colonel Daily sighed as he looked at his empty salad plate. "What I'd give for a big piece of chocolate cake—but I won't get one. I promised Becky I'd try to stay on a sensible diet."

There were no other takers, so Mike returned with a piece of pie and a uniformed first lieutenant.

"Here you are, Colonel—one more for the team."

Pedro "Pete" Ramirez showed even, white teeth in his smile. "Gentlemen—Colonel," he handed Daily a thick accordion file which was tied closed. "The copies you wanted are in there, sir."

"Lieutenant — ah — Manuel Sierra," Daily turned to his former aide. "Do me one last favor and pick up Major Scott at Andrews. Have him back here, Conference Room C, 1530 hours. Sign out a car from the motor pool."

Sierra started to protest. "Colonel, I really wanted to finish—"

Ramirez cut in. "Colonel Daily, if you don't need me for a while, we'll both go." At the Colonel's nod, he spoke over his shoulder to Sierra: "C'mon, *primo.*"

Sierra muttered as he stood and kicked his chair back under the table.

Outside, walking toward the motor pool, he said, "Why did you jump when he snapped his fingers? Don't you realize it's just another instance of *gringos* treating us like peons?"

Pete Ramirez stopped walking and looked hard at Sierra. "We're all on loan, but at the end of this, Officer Daily returns to being a colonel. We're just lieutenants. That's the way the Air Force works. You got a bad attitude, man."

"Bad attitude, huh? At least I'm not a brown-skinned *gringo.*"

Pete stepped closer to Sierra, making him look up to hold his glare. "*En boca cerrado no entran moscas.* Let's go sign out a car."

A closed mouth draws no flies, my ass, Sierra thought bitterly. *I'll remember your attitude, mister. I can stop your next promotion, just watch.*

Lieutenant Ramirez drove, and after they were well started on their round-trip to Andrews Air Force Base, said, "I thought you might fill me in on Colonel Daily. Does he want his men to show initiative, or wait for orders?"

"You're so smart, you figure it out," Sierra sneered, and stared out the window. Pete shrugged and kept driving.

Chapter Six

Mahmud ibn Billah stood silently before Salim Makhadi's fury. When the cell leader had literally run out of both breath and venom, ibn Billah said, "But the infidels, the Americans, have not arrested us. Therefore they must not have the briefcase."

Makhadi thrust his snarling face into Ibn Billah's. Flecks of spit were on his beard and his frog-like eyes bulged even more as he suddenly seized ibn Billah by the throat.

"You fool! You cannot be sure of that!"

Ibn Billah fought his instinct to wrestle Makhadi's hands from his throat, knowing that doing nothing would lower the other man's guard and he could free himself.

For if I struggle, Makhadi will surely kill me. I am far more skilled than he at this type of fighting.

Makhadi shook him, his hands getting tighter, and his thumbs beginning to press beside the younger man's Adam's apple. "Tell me then! Tell me quickly, that you know this to be true—that the American pigs know nothing of our plans!" His foul, panting breath smelled of fear.

Ibn Billah closed his eyes and sagged slightly, pretending to faint. Makhadi pulled his hands away, and ibn Billah quickly turned and leaped over the desk, putting its solid bulk between the two of them.

"Take care who you threaten," he said, and a box cutter glittered in his hand.

Makhadi shook his head. "Again you show your stupidity, to still carry one of those. Throw it away. Our next mission will not need toys such as those."

Ibn Billah clutched the box cutter another moment or two. Then his face changed subtly.

"May Allah grant my next mission truly succeeds." He took a breath, and the box cutter was no longer in his hand. "It must have been the will of Allah our flight was delayed by engine trouble," he mocked the on-board announcement he'd heard while seated on the fifth plane. "Or so said the pilot. Who could have known the pig Americans would get all their planes grounded so quickly? I should even now be in Paradise."

"Allah must have decided you five would be more valuable at a future time. The two remaining pilots even now make their way to our next mission's starting point. They will finish training the next wave of pilots needed." Makhadi was calm now after his outburst.

"Then if I can find that briefcase, *inshallah,* perhaps I might be destined for greater glory also."

"Perhaps," Makhadi said. "But at present you will return to New York and become just another volunteer, still searching the rubble. We have heard that baggage and bodies fell to the roofs of some buildings around the World Trade Center. If this is true, find out where those things were taken and check through them. Keep looking in every possible place for that briefcase until you see your signal ad in their *New York Times.* Your next orders will be in code, in the arts section. You will not return to Lackawanna."

He stopped and looked ibn Billah over, critically; then he turned the lamp on the desk to its brightest light. "You must cut your hair differently and shave off your beard. You will say you are originally from Mexico, a firefighter wishing to help the country which now kindly shelters you and your family." Makhadi curled his lip in contempt. "Gratitude for crumbs! But speak only English or Spanish at all times. They have already arrested men caught speaking Arabic on the phone." He turned the lamp back down.

"Here is a train ticket. You will have a new photo ID once you have shaved. And there is a place for you to live in New York while you search."

With a snap, Makhadi turned the lamp off and vanished as the light itself did.

Ibn Billah stood behind the desk for a few minutes, fumbling the train ticket into his pocket and letting his eyes adjust to the darkened room. A street light outside the window gave just enough light through the blinds for him to find the door. He left the smelly, dirty building and didn't look back, shuffling through the trash on the sidewalks as he walked to the bus stop.

Late that night, the other men who shared the Lackawanna apartment helped ibn Billah shave off his beard and tint his now-naked, badly scarred face a darker tone to match his arms and hands. With much joking, they put a bowl on his head and cut his hair with scissors, making the haircut look as bad as possible.

"Truly your relatives would not know you now," one said, as ibn Billah looked at himself in a small mirror.

"Allah knows my heart, no matter how I change my face," he answered curtly. "I trace my ancestors—even my name—to caliphs and sultans in our glorious history. And they will praise me and be glad for me when I join them in Paradise." But in his own mind, he wondered.

I was beaten for not being devout enough when attending Al Quds, *my mosque when I lived in Hamburg. Yet now the leaders insist I get rid of my beard, which is a man's mark of faithfulness to Allah. Am I being set up? And my face. Now the ruin of it is revealed to those who will stare and ask questions.*

He brushed at the hair sticking to his shirt. *I was indeed markedly handsome. But the scar left by the pig American Special Ops officer shows me hideous, even to my own eyes. Women flinch when they look at me now.*

They took his photo and quickly processed it on a computer, making him a photo ID to hang around his neck.

Now he was just another volunteer firefighter, supposedly of Hispanic descent from upstate New York.

Ibn Billah breathed easier when the train left the station in Syracuse a day later; leaning back against the headrest, he let his thoughts wander. *How fitting I should pretend to be Hispanic. Truly my father had foreseen Allah might make use of me and prepared me well.* He remembered his mother's tears as she begged his father not to take her oldest son with him to Mexico.

"He's only eight years old," she'd sobbed, her very weeping an act of defiance, questioning the absolute rule of his father over the household.

"You have other sons. It is time Mahmud ibn Billah finds what it is to be Moslem in the mockery of a Christian world."

She caught his father's arm. "You did not hate the Christians so much when first we married!"

"When first we married, I was blind. Now I am not blind. I have a diplomatic post in Mexico, and I am sworn to serve Allah in whatever way he wishes to use me." Then with slaps and kicks, he'd driven Mahmud's mother from the room.

His father walked back and grabbed Mahmud's hand. "The servants have packed your clothes. We leave now."

"Father—I—may I say goodbye to my brothers? And my horse?"

His father stared down at him. "Did you not hear me say we leave now? And do not cry, or I will beat you."

Though his chin had trembled, Mahmud hadn't cried, nor had he said goodbye to his brothers or his even more beloved young colt, just broken to saddle.

He'd never seen his mother or his brothers again. But Mahmud rarely thought of any of them, especially after his life abroad began.

As a diplomatic attaché from Iraq, his father lived well. The boy had tutors, and grew up speaking fluent Spanish and English as well as Arabic. He had few close friends of his own age, however. His father preferred his son Mahmud stay by his side, going to meetings and embassy parties.

His father impressed upon him the proud heritage he bore, telling him stories night after night of war heroes and the Prophet. Droning on, his father's voice would eventually put him to sleep.

"Before the Crusades, we followers of Muhammad were the knowledge keepers, the doctors, the scientists. Babylon was the richest city in the world when in our hands. We were the cradle of all civilization in its infancy. We gave even writing to the world. Then other armies came, and the Crusades started. The cursed infidels destroyed all they touched ..."

When Mahmud was fourteen, he and his father made a hurried trip back to Iraq because his grandfather lay dying. They stayed only a month after the funeral, but it was long enough for him to realize his cousins lived in the same miserable poverty the lowliest Mexican workers did. When he dared question his father as to the cause, he found it was again the infidels:

"For who strips our lands of oil to satisfy their greed? Who tries to impose their government upon ours? Who destroys our way of living and of worship?"

In 1982, his father went to the United Nations as a translator, bringing his son to New York, the city nearly sacred to infidels. As a sixteen-year-old, Mahmud ibn Billah was both disgusted by and attracted to the American lifestyle. He saw the last dregs of the hippie "flower children" and thought them pathetic, with their dreams of world peace. The pot he'd tried had no effect on him, but he liked the fast cars and his father's diplomatic immunity to speeding tickets. The loose American women were a bonus, with their Women's Lib silliness.

Ibn Billah sat up straighter in his seat but didn't open his eyes. He'd have plenty of warning before the train pulled into Grand Central Terminal; he could even doze if he wanted. He traced the scar with his fingertips again. *I nearly lost my left eye.* It was almost six years ago; he still recalled the sweet honey of victory turning to dust in his mouth when he realized the men with him had slaughtered the American Special Ops dogs.

I ordered them to leave the infidels alive, so that much information could be extracted from them. But they hadn't obeyed him. In the night, he'd gone from body to body in the tiny, burned-out village, even picking up a leg of one of the soldiers and letting it fall heavily back to the dirt. But no cry came from the dead man and he'd moved on, searching for others. Finally, the last officer was found—and he, praise Allah, still breathed.

They carried their only prisoner back to their base, to "The Spider." Ibn Billah didn't know the man's full name—it was Karem something, and he stopped himself from thinking too long about the raging outburst which had followed. At least ibn Billah had been the executioner of the men who disobeyed his orders and killed instead of capturing the rest of the Americans.

That Karem, even though younger, could still evoke such fear in ibn Billah was something about which he preferred not to think.

When their prisoner was ordered to talk, he'd refused. Karem had administered the first round of torture—but the cowardly American had passed out. Ibn Billah was to stand guard over him and send for Karem when he roused.

Toward morning, ibn Billah woke, startled to hear whispering in Spanish. He crept closer to the prisoner in the dark, dirty hut, listening. To his disgust, the prisoner seemed to be praying to his God, and muttering about his *"querida Anna,"* and his *"hijito."*

A sliver of gray light suddenly slipped into the hut, and ibn Billah jerked back. The American was looking him full in the face, wide-awake, alert. *It was like staring into a mirror. How could an American dog look so much like myself?*

The prisoner opened the neck of his shirt.

"Water," he said. "You must give me water." His voice was slurred, and he groaned.

Ibn Billah curled his lip. *What a weakling. You might resemble me as to my face, but I, ibn Billah, have guts instead of a soft white belly.* He stood, walked two steps and reached for the water bucket at the doorway. When he turned, the American was somehow standing. Something shiny glittered in his hand.

He tried to throw the bucket of water at the infidel, but the American slashed at his face, catching the corner of his left eye and ripping his flesh. Then he grasped ibn Billah's balls with his other hand and twisted.

The Iraqi screamed in real agony, trying to fight off the Special Ops officer and stop the pain in his face and groin. He heard curses and commands from other burned-out houses around theirs, and rifle shots. They were firing into the hut!

Shrieking at them to stop, ibn Billah struck once again at the American and stumbled out of the hut. Only seconds later, when Karem reached the prisoner, the officer was dead.

"I told whoever was shooting to stop," ibn Billah gasped, trying to hold the strips of his face together and see, somehow, out of his eye. Blood dribbled over his fingers and he could smell it. He gagged. His own blood.

"He didn't die from a bullet, fool," Karem said, his voice hardly audible in the clamor. "Sniff at his mouth. You searched him, but failed to find the poison with which he ended his life. You are worthless! Go have your jackal's hide stitched back together—and stay out of my sight."

The train slowed, and ibn Billah leaned down to pick up the small bag he'd placed between his feet. It held only a clean shirt, socks and a razor. It might come in useful if—no, when—the precious, priceless briefcase was in his hands.

At least I have lived to see the day when punishment for the American pigs has begun, even if I had not the glory of helping to deal the first blow. But my time will come. Soon.

Once the train stopped ibn Billah left his seat. He'd never forgotten the name of the Special Ops officer who had cut and destroyed his face, the same name on the new ID card that hung around his neck. It was only fitting that he now entered the heart of his enemy's country as John Ramirez.

Chapter Seven

Faugh, what a stench. Ibn Billah's stomach was queasy again for a few moments when he entered Ground Zero, as they now called the ruins of the World Trade Center. He took his place in the lines of people with their silly plastic buckets.

The way they searched in the rubble for a scrap of human skin, a finger, a bone, was ridiculous to him. They insisted that without something to bury of their dead, their lost ones could not enter heaven.

Stupid infidels. This world itself could be heaven, once the unbelievers are driven from the cradle of all civilization. Let them perish in a hell of their own making. He moved up a little further in line.

After an hour or so, he edged his way out of the bucket line and started toward the water tents. Even the grittiest sandstorm that blew across his homeland didn't choke the lungs like the gray powder he had to search in daily. He was tired of it. He'd been looking for the briefcase for two weeks now, and knew in his heart that it was not going to be found. Allah was not going to smile upon him and place it in his hands. He must have another plan for him.

I certainly have to change my plans frequently. Why didn't Atta order the simpleton hijacker with him on the plane from Portland to leave the briefcase in a locker? Ibn Billah shook his head as he walked. *The young fool must have gotten so excited at being part of the mission that he forgot his orders. However it had happened, the briefcase evidently had been aboard the plane that flew into the north tower at 8:48 AM. The* mujadeen's *names, even that of the simpleton, would be forever reverently recited by schoolboys as they learned their history describing the end of the infidels' world domination.* He sighed. Perhaps he might yet enter those glorious history pages himself.

Now he'd been told he couldn't take whatever he found out of Ground Zero—no one was allowed to leave with anything in their hands. If he did find even part of the contents of the briefcase, he'd have to hide the papers under his shirt. And hope the outbound security people were too tired to be thorough.

Ibn Billah had searched accessible areas at the World Trade Center and nearby buildings hurriedly, while there were still body parts and suitcases in grimy, sickening heaps. Nothing. The few briefcases he'd tracked down, even the one found on the rooftop Makhadi had heard about, were useless. The *al-Qaeda* leaders would have to redraw their plans, and make the timeline fit together again. He knew that not all of the plans would have been detailed in the paperwork in the briefcase. There still had to be men who carried much of the information in their minds and in their hearts.

He pulled off his mask and tossed it into a wastebasket, thinking again of the old man who'd told him to do that when he'd first started. *Was that old Iraqi part of a cell? No one knows who is working on the inside against the infidels. No one but a scant handful of the leaders has any idea of the grandest plans*—or so ibn Billah had realized. He went to the showers. Today he was leaving early.

Later that afternoon, he sat on a floor cushion in the small apartment he shared with four other 'volunteer workers' and spread the *New York Times* out on the floor in front of him.

Eagerly turning to the arts section, he searched for the small ad which would fit into the key he had memorized and tell him when to give up his search, where to report next. He wanted to do something glorious now, to strike back—to repay the Americans for their previous smugness and their stench in death.

He found no ad, and started to fold up the paper so his roommates could search other pages for their instructions—when he paused. An awards ceremony for artists was going to be held next week, which interested him not at all, but the photo and its short article did.

"Anna Ramirez, widow of Air Force Captain John Ramirez (killed while on duty in 1995) will receive the 'Notable Artists—Outside Portfolio Award' next week. Mrs. Ramirez, who usually paints southwestern landscapes, won for her impressionistic oil of orchids. Her 8-year-old son, Maximillano Juan (John) Ramirez, will escort her at the Oil and Pastel Artists Association ceremony and banquet. She is represented by W. R. Perkins Gallery in Albuquerque, NM, which is also the location of her studio."

Ibn Billah sucked his breath through his teeth. *Thanks be to Allah for His infinite wisdom! Here are the wife and son of the American pig whose name I now bear in retaliation for the scar upon my face.* He'd memorized their faces from a photo that had been sewn into the lining of the Special Ops officer's flak jacket. Retribution would be his at last.

The next morning he didn't bother going to Ground Zero. Instead, he called the Artists Association, hoping to buy a ticket to the banquet. On the phone, he assumed the identity of a wealthy Mexican art collector. After a whispered exchange between the young woman who'd answered the phone and someone else, he was told a ticket would be set aside for him at the front desk.

"You may claim it as everyone is being seated, sir," she told him. "And of course we will accept whatever arrangement you wish for the $300."

He thanked her graciously and hung up, cursing viciously after the line had disconnected. *Three hundred dollars! An Iraqi family could live for months on that amount.* Ibn Billah ground his teeth. *These Americans are too rich to be allowed to live. This chance to strike back at the man who ruined my face, when the American's own face was my twin, is not to be lost. I'll buy an expensive suit and shoes too, to look the part of an art dealer.*

He pulled the half-medal and its chain from the small pouch he always carried with him, the weapon with which the infidel had attacked him.

"John Ramirez," he told the medal softly, "I pray there is indeed an afterlife for infidels after all. I will have my revenge while you watch helplessly."

He laid the medal down and stretched luxuriously, thinking. *Anna Ramirez has been without a husband for six years. She should be ripe.* "I will fuck her until her legs bow, and then I will fuck her up the ass so her husband knows she is a whore."

He nodded to himself, planning further. "I will teach her many skills, Captain John Ramirez," he spoke aloud again. "And force her to do to me the things I teach her. Then I will tell her in great detail how I killed you. Your grieving widow has no need to know you actually took your own life—she would consider your coward's death to have been the patriotic thing to do." He put the medal back in its pouch.

"And then I shall kill her."

That night at dinner, two men were missing. Another rushed in just as ibn Billah and his other roommate were silently finishing their meal.

"We are lost!" the man gasped, running to ibn Billah. "The infidels have surely discovered us!"

Ibn Billah felt his heart fumble a beat from apprehension. "Keep your voice down!" he ordered. "What do you babble about?"

"Ramzi and Akbar ibn Hanbal have been arrested—their papers were not in order. If the Americans torture them, they will surely give them our names too. I don't wish to die at the hands of unbelievers." He trembled as he stood beside the table.

"Stop bleating like a sheep, you coward," ibn Billah said. "Americans do not torture prisoners. They feel it is more noble to lock them up and let the other prisoners beat and abuse them." He grinned slightly, enjoying the other man's panic.

He fell to his knees and clawed at ibn Billah's arm. "We must leave, we must escape. We must go home before they catch us."

"Go, then, fool. I remain, *and* remain faithful to my orders. Run away like a frightened little boy." Ibn Billah rose from the table and went down the hall to his bedroom.

Good. Now I have no one sharing my room and no one with curious eyes or prying questions. I will accomplish my own long-delayed revenge.

Chapter Eight

Conference Room C was a secure room with a large viewing screen at one end and a state-of-the-art soundproofing system, which was unnecessary today because of Major Scott's oddly soft voice. Members of his Special Ops squads joked the voice was the only soft thing about him. Every man who'd ever served with him respected him. Most idolized him.

He always handpicked the men who went on a mission with him. And when they returned to the States, Scott treated them to some hell raising. He'd rent an entire wing of a ramshackle motel in the wrong part of town, one where the owners weren't too choosy about guests. And then they'd party for three days with steak dinners and plenty of loud music and beer. After their formal debriefing was over, they'd go back to their regular units. He'd only lost six men in all the missions he'd conducted.

But Scott drove his superiors crazy, both the military and now the desk jockeys for the new Homeland Security office. He annoyed them. No, he irritated the hell out of them.

"Scott?" one of them, an "unnamed source" for many reporters, declared bluntly, "I'll tell you frankly, I don't think the man's a good soldier."

Another from the same office rolled his eyes. "He's a loose cannon. He doesn't seem to understand following orders; he just forges ahead. And why Bill Daily gave him another command—". The rest was left unsaid.

Today Scott stood beside the screen at the head of the conference table. "I'm Doug Scott," he introduced himself. "You guys must already know you've been sheep-dipped." He answered their blank looks. "That just means we're all officially ex-military now, like Colonel Daily told you.

We've all 'resigned' from our posts, and are available for some real hush-hush stuff."

They looked more closely at him. As if to prove his point, he was severely out of uniform, wearing hand-tooled cowboy boots and a denim shirt, which strained across his shoulders. The men waiting for him to speak again were wary. He was a big man—over six feet, more than 200 pounds—and he had a reputation as a hard-drinking, chain-smoking maverick from cedar hacker country down near the border of Louisiana and Texas. A natural leader, his Ops men were fanatically loyal. He put himself in harm's way too, whenever and to whatever he exposed his men.

But he had lost an entire Special Ops squad.

"We report to Tom Ridge, head of the future Homeland Security Department, and you'll find him a fair man, but tough. We've got a hard job to do, unlike anything we've ever tackled before. We can't wait for Congress to approve or fund this before we start to work."

Several of the men around the conference table sat up abruptly. Manuel Sierra was aggressively determined to find fault with anything not precisely military, and now he seized a pen and took rapid notes. Most of the men at the table were 20 years younger than Scott and tempted to dismiss him as a graying geezer, but something about his direct gaze examining their faces stopped them.

And he looked at the men's faces, weighing his impressions of them. "We've got a good team to start with here," he said finally. "I've worked with Bill Daily before. He's personally recommended most of you. Off the record, of course." He cleared his throat.

"Briefly, here's what you'll be doing. Pete, you'll be going cross-country for the next few weeks, recruiting and training truckers for "Operation Storm Watch." Mike and Emad are hauling weather-tracking equipment, pretending to be weathermen themselves. Weathermen. That's ironic:

one of the homegrown terrorist groups in the early 70's called themselves that. Gave some of the boys quite a scare." He grinned without humor.

"We're going to need every pair of eyes and ears we can find to help us. Truckers go everywhere and have to be everywhere—there isn't one state, city or hick town that can do without trucks. And sitting eleven feet up, they see a lot more than anyone on the ground or in a car. Each trucker can be valuable to us. We need every scrap of information we can get."

He put his hands on the polished walnut table and leaned toward them. "I lost the best squad of Special Ops men that ever walked the earth to some of the same bastards that hit us just a few weeks ago. And if you think that sounds like I'm out for revenge—damn right I am. You won't get any more explanation from me. I've always considered self-justification a futile pursuit. But I do know one thing: everybody screws up at least once, including these guys. We're going to be there when they do." He turned away from them and looked at the screen. "Do we have an IT man?"

They looked at each other. Dino peeled himself off a chair and stood up. "I got some computer training."

Scott walked around the table until he was in front of Dino, facing the huge black man, the other men watching them. Scott was a big man, but Dino loomed over him as he did everyone else. Scott nodded.

"Master Sergeant Kenneth Williams, 82nd Airborne."

"That's right, sir."

"You worked with me before. Tehran." He reached out and gripped Dino's hand.

"Yes, sir." Dino's wide grin showed the gap between his teeth and his pleasure that Scott remembered him.

"I begin to understand why this man gets such loyalty from each squad," Emad whispered to Mike.

"Good," Scott said. "Get that computer to zoom in on these photos." He picked up a remote. "Let's run through what we've got."

Half an hour later, there were only a few more photos left. Most of the shots were of crowds, but computer-assisted close-ups brought single faces into focus. Scott told the intent group whatever sparse information he had on each suspected *al-Qaeda, Taliban,* or Muslim Brotherhood member.

Abruptly, Mike said, "Wait a minute." He looked quickly at Emad, who nodded. "Major, Dino, please back up about three frames and zoom in on the four men standing in a parking lot." The photos flipped backwards.

"That one—third one from the right." Mike pointed.

Emad was studying the screen intently. "Remove his beard, and that's the man," he said at last. "Bet on it."

"He was at Ground Zero when we were, just before we found the briefcase," Mike explained. "His scar doesn't show as much with a beard."

A sharp indrawn breath from Pete Ramirez caused both Mike and Emad to turn away from the screen and towards the lieutenant.

"Díos mio," he muttered. *"Mí hermano*—my brother."

Sierra had been lurking and now he pounced. "Your brother is with *al-Qaeda?"* he asked, as if this confirmed his deepest suspicions.

Pete grabbed Sierra's collar in one hand and lifted the little man across the table. "My brother was killed by terrorists," he said slowly and evenly. "He was one of the Special Ops men with Major Scott."

"Just a jackass braying, Major. Pay no attention," Mike untangled Sierra from Pete Ramirez, to the deep disappointment of Emad. He would have rejoiced if Sierra

68

had been flattened. Emad didn't trust Lieutenant Manuel Sierra.

Scott walked closer to the screen. "My God," he said, "Pete, he does look like John. Mike, you and Emad are sure you saw him at the site?"

Sierra had been quieted only temporarily. "Well, we heard the Special Ops men were lured into that village. Maybe *al-Qaeda* has a more attractive bonus program."

He smirked at the tense faces watching him. *Good, that got their attention.*

The Major's hands tightened into fists. Mike stepped in quickly. "Yes, we're sure he was at the site," he said firmly. "He was dressed like a firefighter; he must've been pretending to be one. What in hell was he doing there?"

"I think," Scott said slowly, "he was looking for something."

Scott lay beside the fragile wall of a bombed-out house. He wriggled his body and broken right leg closer to the leaning palm trees, stripped of their crowns and dates by the blast. Sweat ran down his face from the pain and the effort to move silently. He sensed someone coming, and was startled to hear that someone swearing in fluent American obscenities.

"Those bastards! They were supposed to capture the goddam dogs, not kill them. We need information, not bodies."

Suddenly his leg was seized at the ankle, lifted—and dropped. Scott crushed his tongue between his jaws to keep from screaming as his broken bones hit the dirt. Then he bit his hand to keep from retching aloud as the pain rolled over him again.

"They're all dead—this one too. Cursed day that I was given this group of apes to lead! I spit on them!" The voice and its footsteps moved a little off to the side.

He let the ranting get ahead of him and then tried to follow. Scott dragged himself on his elbows, using his good left leg, pushing and pulling his body along the ground. There was no way he could catch up to whoever had been cursing so fluently. But he'd never forget that voice.

He searched for his men for hours, gritting his teeth and waiting for the light-headedness to leave when he tried to crawl too fast. By dawn, he had found only four bodies, identified by a series of tiny beads under the skin, a distinctive pattern for each man. His team always joked about knowing each other's Braille names, but it eliminated dog tags.

I have to leave you here for now, he told each quiet body silently. *God, I hate to do it. But I'll get you out of here. We will come back for you.*

He couldn't find John Ramirez or Mark Allen, two of his very best. *I'm going to make it,* he told himself. *I'll make it out of here, for all you guys. And I'll get even. I swear it.*

A few days later, a chaplain had come to his hospital bed. "Major Scott? They've found the village you described and your squad."

"They're all dead, aren't they?"

The chaplain swallowed, looked away from the gut-deep pain on Scott's face. "Yes. But the worst of it is—the chopper carrying the last two bodies out took enemy fire. It exploded. The next penetration team found only a few charred bone fragments." He hesitated, wanting to be kind but knowing the Special Ops officer neither expected nor wanted kindness. "They've all been declared KIA."

Scott closed his eyes. "Thanks, chaplain. Guess St. Peter needed a crack Special Ops team—and some helo guys too. I'll start calling the families this afternoon."

The phone calls hurt worse than his leg had. He kept hearing the phone ring, and ring, and ring.

"Oh, God," he murmured, "Somebody answer. Answer so I can get this over with."

Suddenly his eyes snapped open, and his hand reached for the clanging clock. His bed was churned up. He'd had the dream again, the replay that had haunted him for five—now six—long years. He drew a shaky breath. The briefing yesterday had brought it all back, in hideous detail. The clock read 3 a.m.—mid-morning in the Middle East.

He got up and lit a cigarette. *No more sleep tonight.* He fought off the despair that always came with the dream, the vision of the faces of his men. The despair was an emotional cancer that killed his energy. But he needed all his energy to do what he had to do.

Turning on the TV, he watched the latest news, sympathizing with the New York police and firefighters, empathizing with their agony as the debris was carted away, bearing microscopic bits of bodies and thousands of crushed lives.

After only a few minutes, he turned off the set. He needed to think.

Scott was not a man who went off half-cocked. His method was the patient accumulation of facts, like ingredients in a recipe. Those facts then sort of marinated in his head until he came up with an understanding of them.

The man with the scar on his face, the operative Mike and Emad had recognized, was the first ingredient.

Chapter Nine

So far his plan was on schedule. Ibn Billah congratulated himself as he shaved, still an unfamiliar operation to him. He'd call Ramirez's widow in another hour or so. Last night had been quite an evening. Success tasted as sweet as ripe, plump dates.

The murmur of voices was quiet behind two enormous hand-carved wooden doors as a very well-dressed man entered the lobby of the Oil and Pastel Artists Association building. He went to the receptionist's desk.

"Buenos noches, señorita. You are holding a ticket for me, no?" ibn Billah queried in a low voice, carefully adding the right amount of Spanish accent.

She looked up. "Good evening, sir. Your name, please?"

"John Ramirez."

Her hand on a heavy, cream-colored envelope, she hesitated, frowning. "Isn't that the same last name as one of the winning artists? Oh, wait, that's the name of the Air Force officer who was killed."

Ibn Billah forced his mouth to smile. "But yes. I am his cousin—we even look alike. He was named Juan José Ramirez, and I was named José Juan Ramirez. Our mothers are very close as sisters," he said, continuing to embellish the lie. How gullible would this young American woman be? "When he was killed, I honored him by taking his name instead. It is traditional in my country, to honor one's relations in this manner. I shall try to speak to Anna, my cousin's widow, after the ceremony. Do you know in which hotel she is staying?"

She smiled. "What a nice tradition, to carry on the name that way. Here's your ticket. Do you wish to use a credit card?"

"No. I prefer to travel with cash, especially in these times," he replied, and he laid three hundred-dollar bills on her desk. Then he placed a small box of very expensive chocolates beside them. "For your trouble."

"Thank you!" She hesitated. He seemed nice, and after all, he was family. "I don't have hotel information here, but if you miss your cousin's widow in the crowd tonight, call me tomorrow. I'll be able to tell you where she's staying."

He'd entered the banquet hall as people began seating themselves. He was polite but reserved with the others at the table. They should have only a vague recollection of "that Hispanic art collector" when the evening was over.

When Anna Ramirez was on stage to receive her award, he applauded. When she told the audience her painting was to be auctioned and the entire amount donated to the WTC victims' families, he led the standing ovation.

Then he worked his way to the front table as the bidding started and gave her small son an envelope. Security guards nodded and smiled, thinking it was an anonymous donation for the fund. He stood beside the boy so his mother could see him, then patted the brat on the back and walked into the shadows of the banquet hall.

Ibn Billah looked at his watch. *I made the little bastard promise to give the envelope to his mother last night at bedtime. The bereaved widow surely opened it to find the photo of her and their son which her American pig of a husband had sewn into his jacket. What devotion.*

He smiled as he walked to a payphone. *What a glorious day. Allah is surely pleased with my plan. I, ibn Billah, will send two more infidels to wherever they go at death. Or perhaps I will simply send the boy to an* al-Qaeda *camp. He is young enough to be retrained.* And the ad in this morning's *Times* had told him to report out west in two weeks. Albuquerque, where the widow lived, was on the way. He'd finish his business there, and report for the next glorious strike at the Americans with perfect timing.

Pete Ramirez stood by a display of CB radios at a truck stop in New Jersey. Dressed in jeans, a leather jacket and a sweatshirt, he looked like most of the truckers who stopped there to eat, shower or rest. He was to meet two brothers who drove team for one of the major van lines. He watched the drivers coming into the restaurant.

Two bearded men ambled in, sturdy-looking, same eye and hair color and set to the jaw. They had to be brothers: one a little older, the other a little taller. Sitting at the counter, they waved away menus offered by a smiling waitress as Pete walked up.

"We know what we want, ma'am," the voice held a soft southern accent.

"What'll it be, gentlemen?"

"Pie and coffee, please," the younger one continued. "Of course, there's only two kinds of pie Ty, here, likes."

"Well, I hope he's not out of luck. What two kinds do you like, Mr. Not-Much-To-Say?"

"Nearly every place has these two kinds, ma'am. I can't believe your fine establishment wouldn't offer them too," the older brother answered, his face serious.

"And those are?"

"Hot or cold," he grinned at her. She rapped his knuckles lightly with her order pad.

"I swear, every time you two come in here, you're up to something. I'll just surprise you—let me get your coffee. How about you?" she turned to Pete, who seated himself beside the younger man.

"Same thing." She rolled her eyes toward the ceiling and went to get their orders.

74

"That your International out there with the dragon etched on the step plates?" Pete gave them the signal.

"Yessir. Our dad's handy with a blow torch," Errol answered. "I'm Errol Lang, from Virginia. This is my *older* brother, Ty, also from Virginia and also named Lang, oddly enough."

"Our mom watched a lot of movies," Ty offered. "He's named for Errol Flynn—"

Errol broke in. "And he's named for Tyrone Power! Whoohoo! What a name!"

Pete chuckled. These men were going to be good to work with—smart, sharp and quick.

They talked quietly, mostly about trucking and the winter weather starting to come on.

"We've always gone home for Christmas," Ty said, when they were standing in line at the register. "But this year's gonna be hard."

"You mean, you know the weather's going to be that bad?" Pete paid for everyone and added a generous tip for the waitress.

"Weather doesn't stop us," Errol said, as he held the door. "It's just gonna be sad. Mom's not doin' well at all."

"Our baby sister worked at the World Trade Center. She won't be home for Christmas," Ty added softly. The three men walked toward the custom blue International.

"I'm sorry," Pete said.

"That's why you can count on us for this Operation Storm Watch team," Errol said, and opened the back door to the sleeper. "C'mon in."

"Yep. We got a fight to finish with them terrorists," Ty added, following Pete into the neat compartment.

Pete pulled a videotape and a small booklet from his jacket pocket. "You guys have a VCR? Good. Just watch the tape and store the book in a safe place."

From another pocket came a cell phone and charger. "Use this to call each time you check in. It's a secure line, and Uncle Sam's paying the tab. You're his eyes and ears out here. Watch and listen. If you come across anything funny, just dial 'O.' Your code name is 'Dragon Wagon.' Thanks, men. Great to have you with us."

Pete drove his old Chevy out of the "Cars Only" lot and headed back onto the Interstate. *Whoever thought to enlist truckers in this team effort had a damn good idea.*

Ibn Billah waited impatiently for the hotel clerk to connect his pay phone line to Anna Ramirez's room. It had been so simple—after reminding the art award banquet receptionist of the lie about being Ramirez's cousin, she'd told him where the widow was staying. Now to set the rest of his plan in motion.

"Hello?"

"Querida. Did you dream about me last night?"

"Who is this?"

"You saw me talking to our son. Didn't he give you the photo, the one I carried next to my heart, sewn inside my flak jacket?"

"The Air Force said you'd been killed."

"I've been in prison camps. Each time I escaped, they caught me," ibn Billah was enjoying himself. He'd written out a script in a notebook, which he followed.

"I don't believe you're my husband."

Tougher than she looked, ibn Billah thought. "Ah, *querida.* Wait until I hold you and kiss you—and our son! You've done a great job raising him."

"It's been hard without you to help," the woman's voice was less crisp, more emotional. Then he heard her begin to cry.

Good, I am getting to her.

76

"Tell me something to prove you're who you say you are."

"We met at the Academy, remember? You were so beautiful, my darling Anna. And you still are. I've missed you—*Dios mio!* I've begged Him night after night to bring me back to you."

Now she sobbed. "John Juan, it is you."

"Yes, your Don Juan," ibn Billah said confidently. "I'm going to come to Albuquerque."

"But I want to see you *now*, John, to hold you and touch you and make sure you're all right—"

"No! We can't meet here in New York. Don't you realize the ones who imprisoned me are the same ones who just destroyed the World Trade Center?" He smiled at the phone. That was no lie. "They might get their hands on me. I can't risk it. They will torture me again. Didn't you see my face?"

"I don't care what you look like. I just want you back, with Mac and me."

"I'll come to Albuquerque. Get my uniform ready and an old military I.D. or passport, if there's one around. That way I can return to work again fast. Anna, I'll see you in a few days. I love you."

He hung up the payphone and looked around carefully. *Good: no one is paying any attention to me.* He threw the notebook into a trash container and kept walking.

Time to catch the train to Trenton, he told himself. *I shall buy a car there. Once I have that uniform and ID, I can go anywhere, to any military base, to any area. For this, I should lead the next operation. I shall have my place of glory, in history.*

Chapter Ten

Scott had just gathered up the last of his papers in his temporary office in Quantico when the phone on the desk rang. He shook his head.

I hope it's not more bad news, he thought. *Finding out another friend of mine was killed at the Pentagon has really torn me up.* He picked up the receiver.

"Scott here."

"Doug, it's Anna. Are you sure John is dead?"

John Ramirez' widow. Has something happened to Mac? His stomach knotted as she described the phone call she'd just gotten. *It can't actually be John Ramirez back from the dead. Can it?*

"Doug? Could John be alive after all? After six years?"

What the hell is going on? He cleared his throat, trying to do the same with his thoughts. "There's not much of a chance, Anna. I know we never got a body back—and that was my fault—but there's no reason to think John could still be alive."

"I'm going to hope that he is, Doug. At least for a few days. He said he'd see me in Albuquerque ..." her voice broke. "His face; his scarred, battered face."

"Don't let him come to your home! I'll set up a secure house where you two can meet. Where's Mac?" He pulled the chair out from behind his desk.

"Right now he's watching TV with my sister Melanie in our suite's living room. I haven't told him anything. But I'm sure he's wondering who that man was, who gave him the envelope for me."

"He talked to Mac?" Scott didn't breathe for a minute.

"I told you, he talked to Mac at the awards banquet last night. Weren't you listening? He gave Mac an envelope

78

that had—" She drew a long breath. "—a photo of me and Mac, the same one I sewed inside the lining of John's jacket. It's a miracle! John's alive and coming back to us!"

Scott reached into his briefcase for his small tape recorder. "Anna, I apologize for making you do this, but let's go over your conversation with this man once more, so I can tape it, for reference. Then we'll decide what we're going to do."

"But Doug, John wants to come home. What do you mean, 'what we're going to do?'"

"If it's John, he'll expect you to follow procedure," Scott cut in. "So I set up a meeting place for you. Can Mac go somewhere for the next few days, until we meet this man and see who he really is?"

Anna hesitated. "I could send Mac on a few days' trip with my sister and her husband on their truck. He'll be safe with them."

"All right." He made more plans as they talked. "We'll re-route your phone calls. Don't tell Mac anything about this; send him with your sister. Don't tell her anything you don't absolutely have to." He thought for a minute. "I guess if this guy goes straight to your home, without calling for directions—we'll have the biggest damn party you've ever seen! If he calls you with some excuse about not finding the house—"

"What!"

"Give him this address and have him meet you there. And Anna, don't be scared. I'll be there when he turns up. Please, please call me every day on my cell phone. It's a secure line, just like this one. My gut instinct tells me there's no way that this guy is John. But I hope against all odds that it is."

He hung up, and thought about the strange phone call.

Is she being stalked for some weird reason? What if it's a twisted art fan who wants her to paint "something just for him"? His thoughts quit chasing themselves for a minute and the knots in his stomach hardened. A face had just appeared in his mind.

I've got a hunch that phone call came from the man with the scar, the fake volunteer Mike and Emad saw at Ground Zero.

It was the second ingredient.

He picked up the phone again. "I want the number of W.R. Perkins Gallery in Albuquerque, New Mexico."

Speaking directly to Winston Rutherford Perkins, Scott introduced himself as an old family friend and told the gallery owner that Anna was being stalked.

"I need you to make sure anyone who calls to get her address is given this phone number instead. Don't allow anyone to give out any more details than that," Scott insisted.

Mr. Perkins' voice on the line was quietly reassuring. "Major Scott, I have heard Anna speak of you. I pledge my word that we will all do our utmost to protect Anna and Mac." The elderly man paused, and then continued. "I shall instruct my staff to be extremely cautious. You probably should know I was an advisor to the French Resistance during WWII. I myself am still on several 'hit lists' around the world. I won't fail in this mission either."

Scott hung up the phone and grinned to himself. *He's a tough old bastard,* he thought. *I'll bet he could tell some stories to make your hair curl. Wonder if he traced a lot of the art the Nazis stole?*

Next he called a special unit at Kirtland Air Force in Albuquerque. "Buck? Good to hear your voice, man. Listen, there's something weird going on, and I'm going to need some help."

Emad put down his pen and stretched his hand, trying to ease the cramps in it. Mike was already asleep in his bunk, too tired to be bothered by the light still on at the Iraqi's desk.

He looked at the stacks of paper in front of him: one stack far too large, the other far too small. He knew there were others who could translate as rapidly as he could. His was the greater worry of accuracy. People from not only his adopted country but also his homeland could suffer terribly if he failed to translate correctly, catching every possible nuance.

He hadn't told Mike about the new fear that accompanied his work.

Twice last week in the late night silence, when he was translating he'd had a vision. Emad had seen his childhood home, so clearly he could almost touch the rough wall his bed had stood next to and smell the saffron his mother always scattered on the sheets to perfume them. He knew his father was in the next room, softly reading aloud the verses of the *Quran* he was studying.

He screwed up his eyes and slapped his face with light, insistent blows. The pleasure of the vision was deceptive and dangerous. It could cause him to miss a word, and if he missed a word, it might change the meaning of an entire sentence. He feared the vision would cause him to make that mistake.

I need to go sniff the air, he told himself, and quietly left the sleeper. Nothing around Double Eagle's workshop looked out of the ordinary.

'Shipshewana,' what an odd name, he thought, walking around the edges of the parking lot. He stopped and looked up at the stars; listened to a dog bark briefly, heard a horse whinny.

81

No big city noises here. He buttoned his jacket. The air had an edge to it as November drew closer.

Odd that he felt so restless. Usually his work was done without emotion. Emad started coughing; the same cough he'd had for several weeks. He breathed out, slowly.

I can see my breath already. And soon it will be much colder. I have not been able to observe Ramadan faithfully this year; that might contribute to my mood. But truthfully, it is the tone and the fervor of what I've translated so far that is making me nearly physically ill.

Whoever had planned the attack on the World Trade Center had also planned more such blows. America's enemies wanted thousands upon thousands of civilians dead, the economy destroyed, and terrified children crying in their beds at night. He sighed.

What is Allah thinking of, that I, Emad Aslam, former Aramaic professor, should be trying to put this puzzle together before it explodes in everyone's face?

The only thing he had so far was that something big was going to happen to the western part of the nation. He and Mike had decided to head west now that their sleeper was completely equipped. He'd work on the translations as Mike drove. And pray the rest of the Storm Watch team would pick up something more definite.

He hoped Pete's trucker recruiting effort was going well. One of his first translations sent to the Department of Homeland Security told of a plan to use trucks to blow up bridges, similar to the Oklahoma City bombing. The truckers he'd met through the years would be madder than hell at the idea they and their trucks could be used for something that underhanded.

Some of the pages from the briefcase proved to be the same plans, only in different handwritings. Apparently those handwritten copies were to go to cell leaders.

They must have feared their mail and email would be watched after the first strike, since they resorted to such old-fashioned ways of getting the plans passed. And the missing pages—what had been written on them? What about the ones crumbled to white dust inside the briefcase?

Again he wondered how the briefcase itself survived the plane's impact and the inferno of the blazing fuel. *Humans certainly didn't, although the hijackers apparently thought at least something of their earthly forms would.* Emad shuddered, and not from the cold.

Atta and his precise instructions for the final care of his body. What an ego, to assume anyone would care what happened to the pieces of such a monster. Did that same ego decide to keep the briefcase with him? Was that how it came through the destruction? Emad's thoughts returned again to that same cold worry.

Who planted that briefcase in Mike's dump truck?

He'd carried a briefcase, too, in his former life. His tiny office at the university in Baghdad was such a far-away memory now.

He had been spared the torture deaths that took his family. He was hurrying home for the feast that ended the fast of Ramadan when a student met him at his car in the university's parking lot.

"Please, Professor, I need help with this assignment. It is too difficult for my muddled brain."

Reluctantly, Emad had delayed, returning to his office and spending a half-hour with the student. The slow student left, grateful for the help, murmuring his repeated thanks as his professor ushered him out of the office. But before he could lock his door, another student had stopped him with a hand on his arm. In a whisper, he'd told Emad about the arrests of the professor's family: his parents, his three younger brothers and their wives at their home. His brothers had been taken directly to Section 7. Their wives

83

had disappeared. His parents had died within a month of each other. And he had slipped into a half-life as a CIA "volunteer."

What irony. I quit teaching, join the CIA to avenge my brothers' deaths, and try to get rid of Hussein—then fight the same old enemies, thousands of miles away from my first homeland. Emad sighed again. *Well, I am still a professor in one small way: I think too much.*

He turned and walked back to the sleeper; put his foot on the first step. *I hope I may die before I am too old and useless to truly help, in this fight or others.*

Chapter Eleven

Many miles away, five kids were sitting crowded together on the curb the next morning. They watched Tyrone, Errol, and the lumpers load the Fowlers' furniture onto their truck. All the movers had heard how much the kids were going to miss Mackenzie and Colin, who were moving to Dallas, where their grandma lived. A plane trip to stay with their grandma during the move had added to their fame.

But the kids staying behind in North Carolina were trying to be cheerful. One of the kids said, "Maybe somebody with seven kids will move in." The others chimed in.

"Or ten!"

"Fifteen kids."

"Twenty-three!"

Ty chuckled as each one tried to top the others. He'd just climbed down the ladder after carefully stacking a lampshade box onto the very top of the tier. Standing on the walk board, he asked, "But what if a little old lady with nine cats moves in?"

They thought that over. Then the smallest girl said, "Maybe she'll know how to bake cookies."

Just then, two men strolled up, each swinging a plastic bag from the grocery store three blocks away.

"Hello, children," one said. They both smiled, but kept walking, nodding to the movers as they passed.

The oldest boy, the usual spokesman for the group, answered, "Hello, Mr. Gopal."

Ty got a drink of water while watching the two men. The kids watched too, until they went into a house five doors down. The oldest boy spoke up again.

"Mr. Gopal said we could call him by his first name because his last name is too hard for us to say. They don't have a car. And they don't have hardly any furniture or stuff. When we went trick-or-treating last year on Halloween, they didn't have any candy, so they gave us dollar bills instead."

"That was neat!" his younger brother broke in.

The smallest girl added, "My Mama says they're going to school to be doctors. She says to stay out of their yard and to keep my puppy out of it too. They talk funny— Mama says they're Indians."

"*East* Indians," the older boy corrected her. "We already asked them, Susannah, and they said they weren't terrorists."

"That's good," Ty said, smiling. "America has room for all kinds of people to live. But terrorists aren't welcome. Aren't you kids getting cold, sitting on the curb like that? Why don't I put some of our furniture pads down and you sit on them?"

It's a damn shame, he thought, unfolding the worn but clean pads for the kids. *Just because someone looks or talks different, they've got people—even kids—watching them now. Those bastards changed our whole country forever, not just New York City.*

"These crazy foreigners," said a trucker, a logger probably, judging by his red plaid jacket. "A friend of mine drove into their so-called Christmas tree farm last week and said, 'When in hell are you going to cut these trees?' And they kind of looked at him, stupid like, and one of 'em finally says, 'For *Christmas,*' like Kenny was the crazy one, right?"

The other truckers in the booth shook their heads. Pete Ramirez, again sitting at a quick-service counter, did too. "Don't they know everybody cuts their trees by the middle of October now?" he asked.

"Aw, it's just another flop for Sonny Boy," the logger continued. "Seems Daddy sends him money to bail him out every time he tries to do something. He's failed so far at a catfish farm, raising sheep, and—let's see, what was it last year? I think the dummy was trying to grow popcorn, or was it peanuts? He wanted to sell snacks at baseball games, he told me." The men listening snickered. "Daddy's some rich oil sheik or something and always sends money to Junior when his latest harebrained scheme dies. He gets in hock to all the merchants around here. Been going on for a couple of years now."

"Hey, something's happened. Turn the TV up!" someone hollered at the waitress. She did so just as the news bulletin began.

"We interrupt our regular programming for this news announcement. Parts of Southern California have gone dark this evening," the announcer began.

No one in the truck stop restaurant moved.

"We have a reporter and camera crew at the San Diego Gas and Electric Office, but security is very tight, and we've been unable to get any word from them so far. Power is out in Escondido and points north. Camp Pendleton and San Onofre are not affected, as their back-up systems came online immediately. Outages are throughout the greater San Diego area, including Poway, Ramona and the Wild Animal Park. We hope to have a full report for you shortly. Please stay tuned."

The trucker next to Pete at the counter blew out the breath he'd been holding. "Jesus, I hope the bastards haven't started on the West Coast now."

Pete tasted his coffee. When he picked up his spoon to add a little more sugar, he noticed his hand was shaking slightly.

Adrenalin rush. I'll give the news people a few more minutes to find out what's going on, he told himself. *Then I'm checking with the Colonel to see what I should do next.*

All eyes in the small truck stop restaurant stayed on the TV screen. The rerun of an old sitcom droned on; the laugh track just as annoying as the first fifteen times the program had been shown.

"Want me to see if I can bring in another station?" the waitress offered.

"Yeah, give it a try, Belinda," one of the cooks hollered. "And turn it up some more. We can't hardly hear it back here."

A couple of bikers from the Harley-Davidson shop across the street slouched into a side booth, their eyes on the TV screen.

Belinda didn't notice; she too was watching the screen, tense. The crawler across the bottom scrolled on:

SOUTHERN CAL BLACKOUT ... NO IMMEDIATE EXPLANATION FROM AUTHORITIES ... ELECTRICITY OFF IN WIDE AREA... STAY TUNED FOR INFORMATION... ANYONE SEEING SUSPICIOUS PERSONS OR MOVEMENTS AROUND POWER STATIONS ASKED TO CALL LOCAL POLICE IMMEDIATELY... AUTHORITIES URGE EVERYONE NOT TO PANIC... STAY TUNED FOR DETAILS.

The game show on that channel resumed, then was abruptly interrupted again.

"An electric generating plant in Southern California has gone off-line, leaving a wide area without power. Please do not call the area for information, as phone lines have been overwhelmed at this time." The on-screen reporter took a breath. "Camp Pendleton is on Highest Alert. The nuclear facility at San Onofre has not been affected; its auxiliary power supply came on immediately. Escondido, El Cajon, San Marcos and other communities in the area are affected. Authorities are urging people to stay calm, remain in their homes and to use their battery-powered radios from their earthquake kits for updates. Our network affiliate has a crew on its way to the area and we'll continue to monitor this situation. We now resume our program."

Belinda looked away from the screen and turned the volume down a little. "Oh, hi, Wolf," she reached for two menus. "I'm sorry. I didn't see you and Mazman Frank come in."

The bikers shrugged. "No problem," Wolf said.

"What's going on?" Mazman Frank asked her as she walked up to their booth.

"Nobody knows for sure," she answered. "What'cha gonna have?"

"Or nobody's talkin'," the trucker next to Pete at the counter muttered.

"You think it's terrorists?" Pete asked him, just to start him talking and get his take on things.

"I don't know what I think," he said. Then he turned to face Pete. "But I do know if I ever get a chance at those bastards, I'll kill 'em." Several other truckers seated around them within hearing distance nodded, quietly agreeing.

Be easy to get a little more help around here for "Storm Watch," Pete thought. I'm going to stay overnight anyway. I want a good look at that Christmas tree farm.

Truckers were finishing their meals, getting ready to move on. News or no news, they had deliveries to make and deadlines to meet. Pieces of conversation swirled around Pete as he ordered his dinner.

"Weather Channel says six inches of snow possible by morning..."

"Hell, I ain't puttin' on those damn chains for that. I'll just wait. By the time I get chained up, the plows will have been out two or three times."

"Hold it!" a voice called out. "Turn up the TV again!"

"We now have a report about the power blackout in Southern California. We go to our affiliate reporter on the scene."

"Good evening, everyone; this is Wendy Jackson. We have information on that energy blackout. Older equipment, which is in the process of being replaced, failed this afternoon, before the new equipment was on-line. Authorities have assured us the power outage was not due to any terrorist action. Crews have just about finished their work, replacing the old equipment with the new, and full power should be back on in most areas within the hour. Electricity has already been restored to Escondido and most points north. Again, we repeat, the power outage was not due to any terrorist action. We now return you to your regular programming."

Truckers began paying their bills and leaving. Belinda, now at the cash register, called to Pete. "You need some more coffee?"

"No, I'm good, thanks," he answered. *I'm still going to check in with Colonel Daily,* he decided. *I'll call him when I get to a motel room.*

Not long afterward, he opened the door to his room and went inside, turning on the lamp and locking the door behind him.

First, I call Colonel Daily, then a long, hot shower and bed.

Even though none of them was supposed to be in the military now, technically anyway, Pete still thought of the older man as "the Colonel." He couldn't figure out why

Manuel Sierra had such a grudge against the ranking officer.

I haven't seen him treat anyone any differently, Pete thought, pulling a few things out of a small suitcase. *Sierra's got a chip on his shoulder the size of a plank. Doesn't make sense. And neither does that 'tree farm.' Tomorrow I go snooping.* He chuckled to himself. *I hope I can be James Bond instead of Inspector Clouseau.*

In the living room of his small house, Karem turned off his radio. *The infidels have had only a taste of the darkness they will soon encounter.* He said his evening prayers and then sat at his desk.

The time for our actions is growing closer. He stroked his beard, thinking: *I cannot find a flaw in the plans. The detonators are completed, the supplies portioned out and ready to be assembled into bombs. Truly, the only remaining questions are when? And who is to be appointed the leader of the operation?* He had assumed he would be, but so far, no word. The Director had not yet said. Karem sighed.

I am weary of this world, he thought. *Inshallah, I wish to be at peace, in Paradise. And before the New Year dawns.*

Idly he watched a spider crawl across a corner of his desk. *That is a good omen.* He laughed softly; he was proud of his nickname and that the mention of it frightened grown men. "I have indeed woven a strong web," he said aloud. "And thousands of American flies will be trapped in it."

Chapter Twelve

Ibn Billah peeled bills from a roll of money, watching the auto salesman licking his lips without realizing it. *Greed makes so many people stupid,* he thought. *He looks just like a mongrel cur drooling over a bone.*

"You'll take care of the registration change and license and so forth?" he asked the man.

"Sure," the salesman answered, fascinated, as the pile of hundred-dollar bills on the desk grew taller. Sixty of them made a nice stack. "I'll get you a receipt. The tag on the car's good for two more weeks anyway. Sorry the sales manager's out to lunch, but I can fix you right up."

Ibn Billah pressed another hundred-dollar bill into the other man's hand. "For your trouble, *señor,*" he said, smiling. "Now I will be able to get to my relatives in Mexico City without them worrying about me flying."

Probably the most money this dirty little place has ever seen, he grinned to himself, as he drove out of the used car lot. It was in a bad area of the city; he went a couple of miles to a better neighborhood and stopped for gasoline.

And I need something to eat. I won't find a meal I would enjoy; but perhaps I may order something I can tolerate. He turned the old red sports car into the driveway for a fast food place.

He had his map and the route highlighted in yellow on it. He found his way out of the Trenton neighborhoods and onto Interstate 95.

I-95 to 85 and then I'll get I-40 from Durham, North Carolina.

He pushed a cassette into the player on the car's dashboard. Lola Beltran's voice poured forth, the lyrics in Spanish, the music behind her full and lush. He started up the ramp.

If I must appear Hispanic, then I shall also have the pleasure of some of their best music. He jammed down the accelerator and used the shoulder to roar around an eighteen-wheeler on the right side, cutting back in front of the truck. The trucker hit his air brakes and horn at the same time; Ibn Billah held his left hand out the window, middle finger extended.

"Fuck you," he said, rolled the window back up and turned on the car heater. He was enjoying himself; it'd been too long since he'd been behind the wheel on an open road.

Seven a.m. in Flagstaff and Pete Ramirez had just started into a little café in town when he stopped and squinted against the brightening rays of sunlight.

Maybe it's snow-blindness. It can't be—yes, it is.

Tony Parker Chino strode across the snow-crusted parking lot and took the door handle away from his friend. "Are you going in, or just letting all the warm air out, Pete?"

Over plates of *huevos rancheros,* Pete and Tony began catching each other up on their news. They'd roomed together at Northern Arizona University before Pete was appointed to the Air Force Academy. Tony, a Native American from Acoma Pueblo in New Mexico, stayed in Flagstaff and finished his degree in forestry. Then he'd become a smokejumper, traveling throughout the U.S. fighting the worst forest fires.

"I hurt my ankle in the last one, though," Tony told Pete, and held his coffee cup up so the waitress could refill it. "Shattered it. Got enough pins in it to knit my own socks. Thanks, Lois. Where's Kathy today?"

"She's pulled room mother duty for her youngest," she answered. "Helping them rehearse their Thanksgiving play. Oops, sorry, Tony. Us Pilgrims forget how touchy you redskins are," she giggled.

"Me no redskin," Tony frowned. "Me tan skin. You color blind?"

Pete grinned and shook his head. "Did the Dean ever forgive you for that war dance you did around the pep rally bonfire?"

"Sure he did. I told him it was your idea," Tony chuckled. "But how's everybody in your family? How's John? And your beautiful sisters?"

Pete looked older suddenly. "John was killed in the Mideast just a short time after I got to the Academy. Terrorists attacked ambushed the entire squad. The leader, Major Scott, played dead, and then tried to find John and the rest of them—or at least all their bodies—but he couldn't."

Tony looked into his friend's face. Pain and anger were in his eyes still. He remembered how Pete had idolized his big brother, wanting to follow in his footsteps: the Academy, Special Ops—to be just like John.

"I'm really sorry, Pete. How are your folks doing?"

"Well, it happened five, no, it's six years ago. My Mom's actually taken it better than Dad did. But they're both okay. And my nephew comes out to the ranch every summer. Mom stays in close touch with Anna, John's widow."

They talked a little while longer; then Pete said, "What are you doing nowadays?"

"Looking for work, now that my ankle's healed as much as it's going to. I could get a desk job at the Forestry Department—but I couldn't stand being indoors all the time. Why? You need a partner for something?"

"Maybe I do." Pete filled him in on the suspicious-sounding tree farm.

Tony's long face assumed a grin that made him look like a hungry wolf. "Now, you can't expect me to go on down the road like some tourist when you're up to your

94

Mexican rear end in something hot. You see, I'm bored, old man—bored glassy-eyed. You may have the immediate solution to this poor Indian's boring life."

"Why me, Lord?" Pete rolled up his eyes in pretended resignation. "Why do I always have to pay for Wounded Knee? All right. Why don't I go in the front door and pretend to be a tree buyer, while you slip around behind the scenes and find out whatever you can? And try not to fall over your own feet back there."

"A sneak and peek, huh?" He sighed loudly. "You Mexicans always leave the tough stuff to us. Of course, you couldn't sneak up on a deaf granny sitting in her rocking chair."

"And why not?"

"Your spurs rattle too loud, *vaquero*."

Pete stood in the front office of the Christmas tree farm waiting for the manager. There was no receptionist—instead, a nervous boy of fourteen or fifteen was trying to fill and start an ancient coffee maker.

A door opened and a young Middle Eastern man came into the room. He was smiling and cheerful. "Good morning! May I help you?"

"Are you the manager?"

"Yes, and I am the owner of this wretched place also. I am Jafar Al-Rimi. If you are hoping to buy peanuts I regret to tell you our crops failed last year."

"That's too bad. Actually, though, I was hoping you hadn't sold all your Christmas trees yet. I'm a department store display designer from Santa Fe. We bought trees earlier this year for our store displays, but the truck got routed wrong and our trees ended up in Florida. We need replacement trees ASAP. How many can you sell us?"

A crash behind the two men, and the coffee carafe was in glistening glass shards on the tile floor. The teenager ran from the room and returned with a broom and dustpan.

Jafar Al-Rimi shrugged. "My sister's son. That's the fourth coffeepot he has broken in six weeks. Your department stores do not happen to sell unbreakable coffee pots?"

Pete shook his head. "Nope. If we did, I'd buy one myself. Are all your trees sold?"

"Most of them are," Al-Rimi said. "Come, let us go into my office and talk of this. How many do you need?" He opened the door and started to usher Pete inside and to a chair.

"At least a hundred, maybe more."

Al-Rimi's entire face drooped. "Alas, we have not that many left over. If you only needed four or perhaps five, even ten, we could gladly help you. But a hundred? No, I am sorry. 'An empty hand has nothing to give,' Mr.—ah—what did you say your name was?"

"I'm Pete Rodriguez."

"Mr. Rodriguez, I am sorry," Al-Rimi said firmly. "You must look elsewhere for your trees."

"It was worth a try," Pete said, and walked away from the inside office door. "Thank you for your time, Mr. Al-Rimi. Careful—don't cut yourself," he said to the teen, still trying to pick up bits of glass.

He walked outside. He knew he hadn't given Tony enough time to do much of a snoop job. He'd have to pull the "car trouble" trick, and make it a good show. He got behind the wheel and turned the ignition to "Accessory," clicking the key several times. Naturally, the motor didn't start.

Cursing loudly so they could hear him in the office, he got out of the car, slammed the door; kicked the car's left front tire. He knew someone was bound to be watching him. He yanked up the hood.

Good thing I drove my old clunker as part of my "blending into the background" plan, Pete thought. He took off the wing nut on the breather, lifted off the cover and took out the air filter. He wedged open the butterfly valve on the carburetor with a small wrench..

Al-Rimi was suddenly at his elbow. "What is wrong with your car, Mr. Rodriguez?"

"Aw, it gets stubborn on cold mornings," Pete answered him. "I bet it's flooded again. It'll take about a half-hour to get over it. Can I wait in your office? It's cold out here." He knew Al-Rimi would be bound by the strict rules of Middle Eastern hospitality.

"But of course," Al-Rimi said, clenching his jaw. "I will wait with you. We have found another coffeepot, and I shall offer you a cup while your car recovers."

"Thanks," Pete followed Al-Rimi back inside. *This will give Tony time enough for a good look behind the scenes. Too bad I don't have any photos of kids or my big fish to pass the time.*

Chapter Thirteen

"What in hell was going on back there?" Mike asked Emad as they pulled onto the Interstate, heading west out of Indianapolis.

"A couple of other truckers decided I looked like a terrorist," Emad said quietly. "I'm getting too old for this stuff. Years ago, I wouldn't have had a problem talking—or fighting—my way out of anything."

"They weren't listening to what anyone had to say," Mike responded grimly. He'd had to shove one trucker away from Emad, who'd been backed into a corner and surrounded by five or six men. The angry trucker had been bellowing something about "damned camel jockey" and shaking a fist in Emad's face. Younger and much bigger than the Iraqi, the other driver looked like a bull-hauler, with his western boots and hat with the rattlesnake hatband.

After Mike shoved the other trucker aside, he'd stood beside Emad and said, "We've driven team for over ten years. He doesn't ride a camel—he drives an International. Anybody got a problem with that?" At six foot two, Mike could look big and mean when he chose to, and he chose to this time.

The other men had drifted off, especially when the truck stop manager came running up. The angry trucker got in one last slam: "I better not catch you ever squealin' to any damned terrorist, mister." He turned and spat on the floor at Mike's feet. "You don't scare me. Be sure you keep your 'good buddy' in line," he snarled, and left.

"Well, I'm glad they weren't listening," Emad continued, as Mike shifted and the truck picked up speed.

"What? Why?"

Emad fluttered his eyelashes at Mike and ducked his head. "Because then everybody would know I was your 'good buddy.'"

"Go take a flying leap," Mike said, grinning. But the incident bothered him, especially that night when he was trying to get some sleep.

The best thing is for me to go in alone and pay for the fuel, he decided. *Everybody's still jumpy. Might as well give 'em time to get over it. If Emad stays in the truck, we should stay out of trouble.*

Back at Pete's motel room, Tony was sketching a rough map on a piece of paper.

"There's a big bunkhouse here," he pointed, "and then just about, say, twenty feet left or so, there's some Quonset huts. Five of 'em, all neatly lined up, with the doors padlocked and the windows painted over."

"Locked against what?" Pete asked.

"Plane thieves, I guess," Tony answered. "At least that was all there was in the one building I had time to break into—four light planes, like you'd use for crop dusting or something."

"So if each of those other buildings holds that many planes—why would a Christmas tree farm need twenty crop-dusting planes?"

"No idea. But your Colonel might have some ideas about it. You gonna call him?"

"I don't have anything more than what you found out to report. We can't have the FBI or some other agency arrest this Al-Rimi just because he can't stay in business. For all we know, he really could be the ne'er-do-well son of a rich oil sheik. And we can't afford to antagonize any OPEC members right now." Pete sighed. "I don't know what to do. Guess I'll call the Colonel anyway. I'd like to recruit you as part of the Storm Watch team permanently, even if you're not a trucker."

"I can get a *Trucking for Dummies* book and read it."

Pete snorted and dialed the phone.

Manuel Sierra answered.

"What are *you* doing in the Colonel's office?" Pete demanded.

"I haven't gotten an assignment yet," Sierra said bitterly. "You got to take off and start glory-hunting. Me, I got to step back into my old job, Mr. Peon to the Colonel. I was supposed to be on the road by now, with my own rig. I'm going to talk to my mother's brother, the general. I'm sick of this shit. What do you want?"

"I need to talk to Colonel Daily."

"He's not here, *tonto*. Tell me what you need."

Sierra jotted down notes as Pete Ramirez talked. "You get all that?"

"Yeah, yeah. Or should I say, 'S*í, sí, mí hermano*.'"

"Will you see that Colonel Daily gets my report when he's back in his office?"

"You want me to type it in triplicate and stamp it 'Top Secret' too?"

"Come on, Sierra. It might be important."

"I'll take care of it." Sierra hung up the phone and looked at his notes. "Lieutenant Suck-up's blown it this time for sure," he sneered to the empty office.

Sierra was an avid collector of injustices and betrayals, keeping them fresh in his memory. He was sure there was an organized plan to delay his career advancement so he'd stay a flunky in Daily's office. He couldn't find out what the hell they were doing with all the money funding the project. Whoever they were, they knew that if he got out of the office he would soon find out what was happening. And now this 'important' report from Ramirez.

Important, my ass, he thought. *Why should I work to advance the reputation of Pete Ramirez?*

"There's nothing here," and he tossed the notes into the wastebasket. "God, will I ever get out of this damn office!" He leaned back in his chair, fingers laced behind his head.

I'm sick of lying low and waiting. Either I'm going to get some advancement, or they can have someone else do their snooping. I've looked through old files until my eyes feel like they're boiled. I think I'll tell them they either come up with some real money, or I go talk to someone who would be interested.

Ty and Errol were rolling out of Durham, North Carolina, their van loaded, each shipper contacted, and delivery schedule set.

"We got just enough time to get back from Phoenix for Thanksgiving at home, after we get Dallas, Las Cruces and Tucson off," Ty said, looking at their paperwork.

"That'll work out," Errol said. "And we'll stop at the Diamond B in Phoenix; they've got the best food of any of 'em. Makes my mouth water just thinking—what in blazes?"

An old red sports car had whipped around them, flashed past in the left lane—and then they saw its left rear tire blow a second before they heard the explosion.

"Hang onto it!" Ty yelled, even though the other driver couldn't hear him. He grabbed the CB mike. "We got a four-wheeler out here on I-40, just about mile marker 153. He's blown a tire and he's fighting the car; an old red sports car, to stay on the road."

"I heard you, driver," a voice came back. "You in that furniture van ahead of me?"

"Yeah, he's to our left."

"I see him. He's doing pretty good holding onto it. Thanks for the warning, though. Slow down, everybody. If he loses the wheel, we don't wanna run over what's left of him."

Errol began slowing their rig too, and just as he did, the sports car left the passing lane and moved in front of them. The flapping tire was finally having a braking effect. The car kept slowing, crawled onto the shoulder, and stopped.

Errol parked the brothers' rig right behind the car. They got out and ran to the driver's side. He looked at them a minute or two, dazed, and then began laughing.

"Hey, man, I got *cojones*! Did you see that driving?" he bragged, getting out of the car.

Ty put his hand on the driver's shoulder. "Don't walk too close to the traffic! Are you okay?"

"Get your hands off me, *cabrón*!" The driver was instantly furious. "I drive better than an Indy 500 driver can freakin' do and all you can say is, 'Don't get close to the traffic!' Get out of here and leave me alone!"

"Gladly," Ty said through gritted teeth. He and Errol walked back to their truck and started it up. "Guy's nuts," he said as they pulled out onto the Interstate again.

"He'd have to be, to laugh like that after a blowout," Errol agreed. "But we did the right thing by stopping to check on him."

"Sure an ugly SOB," Ty continued. "You see that scar on his face? The whole left side's messed up."

"Yeah. With his attitude, I'm not surprised. He probably starts barroom brawls for the fun of it."

Chapter Fourteen

Ibn Billah paid the tow truck driver in cash, grudgingly adding a tip.

"Thanks, mister," the driver said, and left ibn Billah and his sports car at a tire dealer's garage.

"I'll go eat while you change the tire," ibn Billah told the shop foreman. "And put a spare in the trunk too." He walked across the street to a small restaurant.

I still drove better than anyone else could have, he told himself. *I am an expert driver. Surely Allah smiled, to see such marvelous driving.*

He dug some change out of his pocket and got a newspaper out of the machine at the front door.

Seated at a table and told that his dinner would take about twenty minutes, he unfolded the paper.

I may as well see what new ghost the infidels are chasing now. Today's date—this would have been my father's birthday. But he had no idea what age his father would have been; he had died in the bombing of Baghdad during the first few days of Desert Storm in 1991.

He hadn't been with his father in Baghdad. He'd been in South America—training, recruiting, training again. His father had been proud of his son's loyal service to *al-Qaeda,* predicting his son would rise through the ranks to a position of great importance. Yet Mahmud ibn Billah had been passed over again and again. His father had written letters, contacted men he knew, cajoled and even bought favors and information when necessary. Mahmud had served, and served well, for nearly twenty years.

Too bad the World Trade Center buildings didn't crumble on the same date my father died; that would indeed be a memorial. Foolish man. If he hadn't gone to Iraq to see "a friend of a friend" about that long-delayed promotion for me, he might have lived to see those towers in the dust. But only Allah knows each man's allotted time.

He grinned behind his newspaper. *Wait until I have killed the pathetic widow of that Special Ops dog who ruined my face. I will first have her, and then his old uniform and papers—I shall also bring his matchstick-legged son with me. What a recruit for* al-Qaeda. *And when I report to my new post in the west, with my uniform on and my new identity, and I may walk into any military base in America, unchallenged—I shall be praised and honored by everyone, even the Director.* Ibn Billah laughed out loud. Then he realized the waitress was standing beside him.

She smiled as she refilled his water glass. "It's good to hear someone laugh again," she nodded towards the paper he'd quickly folded. "I always enjoy the comics too. I'll go get your dinner now," and she went towards the kitchen door.

He quieted his ragged breathing. *She has no idea what I am thinking,* he assured himself. *I am far too clever for these stupid Americans. Someday, someday very soon, all of them will remember my name. I will be in their disgusting fat, lazy children's history books forever.*

"As soon as we crossed the Mississippi River, we were in 'the west,' Emad," Mike said.

The Iraqi shook his head. "That doesn't help me pinpoint the location of the cell that's due to activate next."

"I know. But I only understand some military terms in Farsi; I can't read Arabic script. I can't help you at all." And Mike stared out of the sleeper window, beating a fist rhythmically on the windowsill.

Emad looked closely at him. *Now he's showing his age,* he thought. *The stress has him looking less like a basset and more like a Shar-pei.* He cleared his throat, then coughed. When he got his breath back, he said, "Somehow we'll get these bastards. Bet on it."

They were parked at a truck stop outside Amarillo, Texas. Mike was methodically contacting every team member this morning by email. He'd been concerned over an odd message from Pete Ramirez. Pete had gone to Colorado Springs to recruit a husband-wife team, Allen and Elaine Coe. Their truck kept rolling: Allen liked to drive in the wee hours, and Elaine was cool and calm in the worst traffic. They'd be able to log many more miles than any of the others—watching; listening, hauling their usual high-tech loads but always alert for any tiny piece of information.

But then Pete had said something to the Colonel about going back to Flagstaff, because he wanted to find out if a tree falling in the forest made a noise if no one was there to hear it. And he'd referred to the Colonel as his "philosophy professor."

Mike was still puzzled over that one. *Someone must've been openly listening to Pete when he called in. What did he mean?*

"I think we'll go on to Albuquerque for tonight," he told Emad. "That'll give everyone time to get to their laptops and fill all of us in on what's happening. Pete may be on to something. I sure hope so."

Doug Scott frowned at Anna Ramirez. "The last time you heard from this guy, he was in Knoxville. He should be here in two days at the most. I don't want you trying to be Supergirl and catch this guy by yourself."

She matched his glare. "And I don't want a bunch of eavesdroppers watching while I'm saying hello to my husband who's been missing for six years."

"Anna, we don't know that this guy's John."

"We don't know that he isn't," she said stubbornly.

Scott shook his head. "We've been over this a dozen times. God knows I'm still hoping that it is John. He was my best friend too." Scott was pleading. "But you've got to be sensible and not take stupid chances. You think John would forgive me if I let anything happen to you? After I—" he stopped, cleared his throat. "After I let him and the whole squad down?"

Anna's glare softened. "You still figure somehow it was your fault."

"I'm the only one who got out alive."

"Doug, nobody blames you. I don't. The other wives don't. The kids don't."

"I look at the guy who blames me every morning in the mirror when I shave. And it *is* my fault, Anna. I'll carry this guilt to my grave. The only good thing is that coffins don't have mirrors inside. But I know there'll be mirrors in hell. Lots of them."

She walked over to him and put her arms around him, then held him tightly.

"Let it go, Doug." After a long pause, she said softly, "You believe there's not a chance this man is John. But I think he is. And I'm going to continue believing that."

Preparations went on at the safe house the rest of the afternoon. A crew from Kirtland Air Force Base, under the supervision of a Major known only as "Buck" worked swiftly, checking out the hidden camera system and the listening bugs throughout the rooms in the small two-bedroom house. Then the crew packed up and left.

Anna looked at Scott. "Mac left this morning with Melanie and Lucas."

"I hope you told your sister as little as possible."

"Yes. By the way, her husband hauls a lot of secret stuff. He's got a 'Q' clearance too."

106

"Good. Now, you know I'll be outside with another officer when you open the door to this guy. Better yet, unlock the front door and then come back into the kitchen, closer to the back door."

"Right. And I'm to make sure it isn't John—" Anna had an unreadable expression on her face. "And then I call you in by saying, 'Are you hungry? Can I fix you something to eat?' Like I'm June Cleaver."

Scott nodded his head. "Yeah, yeah, I know. But that'll be our signal to come through the back door into the kitchen, and then we'll nail him. Maybe he has some useful information. That's the only reason I'm not going to shoot him on sight."

"I stay here in the kitchen until you've caught him."

"Right. If he didn't obviously know what you looked like—" Scott stopped, remembering the intimate details of the last phone conversation Anna had with this imposter. He'd listened, unwillingly and embarrassed, to the entire tape of their "pillow talk" conversation.

He continued, "I wouldn't let you be the bait. I'd have another woman play your part."

"Better yet, get Dennis Rodman to play me."

Worried as he was, Scott chuckled. "You're something else, Anna. God, I wish I'd seen you first."

"You did. You dated me before John did."

"Yeah, but I was such a dumb ass I didn't realize just what an incredible woman you are."

Scott left the house; walked around the block to an unmarked van and got in the passenger side.

"Why don't you take the van up to Blake's and get us some burgers? Have them put green chili on mine," he said to the officer inside. "Then we'll both camp out in the back yard. I don't trust this guy at all." He got out of the van and started back to the alley behind the house.

107

Anna sat in the living room of the safe house for a few minutes, searching for her regular newscast on the unfamiliar TV. She missed Mac already. "It's a good thing Doug isn't planning on shooting on sight," she said aloud. "John would get really ticked if his best friend opened up on him just as he walked in the door. I wish he could get here sooner. We've got six years to catch up on."

She'd started to eat a sandwich when the phone rang. *Must be Doug again,* she thought. *He's getting worse than any old mother hen ever could be.* She left the kitchen and hurried back into the living room.

"Hello?"

"*Querida,*" the voice breathed.

Anna gasped. "John? John Juan, where are you?"

"I'm going to stop for a few hours' sleep in Oklahoma City, my dearest, but I shall be clasping you in my hungry arms very soon." Ibn Billah smiled at the phone. "Your Don Juan will soon be taking you to the heights of ecstasy, my gorgeous one." He turned and looked at the billboard near the pay phone he was using; something about the best western wear in Amarillo. *I shall be in her bed sooner than she even dreams. And then her last dreams will be nightmares indeed.*

"Some phone system you've got," she greeted Doug as he came in the back door.

"What do you mean?"

"John just called me; he said he's staying for a few hours in Oklahoma City to sleep and then he's driving on in. But Caller ID said the call came from Amarillo."

"The bastard! He's trying to slip in on you!"

Anna shook her head. "Don't call my husband a bastard, Doug; I don't care how good a friend you are. And John can come in any time he wants."

"Did he ask you where you were?"

"No. He knows where home is. He's coming home, home to me. And I'm not there. Because of your denial, because of your paranoia, my husband is going to come home to an empty house. I hate you!"

"Your home isn't empty," Scott said grimly. "Mac's dog is there, and a Special Ops officer. If it is John—and I still don't believe it is—that officer will bring John here— to you."

She turned her back on him and he heard her sob. "Don't reason with me like I was Mac's age! The love of my life is coming home, and you won't let me go to him. Get out of here! You and your damned 'standard procedure.'"

He went out to the back yard again, and called Anna's real home. "This is getting really strange," he told the other officer. "She's positive this guy's her husband. Keep a sharp lookout. I'm going to call Buck and have him send another man or two as back-up for here and for yourself. I'm not taking any chances with this guy."

Ibn Billah left Amarillo after eating, passing the rest of the truck stops and fast food places.

I shall be in Albuquerque in five hours; by midnight, he told himself. *She thinks I'm still in Oklahoma City; how gullible this woman is! But she should be a tasty treat. Perhaps I may extract other information from her before I kill her, while she writhes under me on the bed. Maybe I should put on her dead husband's uniform before I take her.*

Mike waited patiently for the traffic to clear before getting back onto I-40, letting the last of the pack, an old red sports car, go by, and then he merged into the lane.

"So what would be your best guess about where they might hit next?"

Emad took a few minutes to answer. "I don't know with any certainty. Logic tells me the next place they will strike is the West Coast; Los Angeles, probably. It's a huge population area, and very wealthy, to the rest of the world."

"We heard from everyone except Pete Ramirez," Mike said. "It could be he's really on to something; we'll just have to wait and see. But I have a hunch that you're right, whether you're going by logic or what you've translated so far. California would be a very likely target for *al-Qaeda.* I thought for a while that power outage was their handiwork."

"Glad it wasn't. So we are going there?"

"'Go west, young man, go west,'" Mike quoted Horace Greeley. "And old codgers—that's us—can continue to head that way, too. I just hope we can warn everyone to pull the wagons into a circle before the attack."

A small black car merged onto the Interstate and the driver flipped on the cruise control, staying three cars behind the Environmental Solutions rig.

"Why don't I call some of my relatives to come over from New Mexico and we'll stage an Indian attack on this Christmas tree farm?" Tony suggested, as he and Pete sat in their motel room in Flagstaff.

"Ha, ha," Pete replied, absent-mindedly. He was still studying the rough map Tony had drawn yesterday after snooping through as much of the operation as he could.

"I'm surprised you haven't heard from Colonel Daily."

"I am, too," Pete answered. "In fact, it kind of worries me. I had to sound like a Middle Eastern philosophy student on the phone with Sierra when I realized the two tourists at the counter were listening to me. Maybe he thought I was drunk or something. Or just kidding."

"Does he know you as a kidder?"

Pete shook his head. "No, as a matter of fact, I've taken my Special Ops career seriously, especially after John died. It's not something I kid about."

"Then call him again. Maybe something happened and he hasn't gotten back to the office yet to read the notes your non-friend wrote for him."

Pete blew out a deep breath so his voice would steady. He was furious.

"Well, Colonel, I'm glad I called you again. If I ever get a chance to punch Manuel Sierra when he's out of uniform, I'm gonna do at least that with the utmost pleasure." He listened intently to the phone for a few minutes.

"Yes, I can, Colonel," he replied. "As a matter of fact, I'd gladly put my life in Tony Parker Chino's hands if it came down to it. I trust him totally. And he's already done a little work for us. Let me fill you in on what you didn't get from Sierra."

When he hung up, he turned to Tony. "You're in," he said, grinning. "But the Colonel can only pay your room and board for now; he has to get all the paperwork and authorizations through before you can draw a salary."

"Okay by me," Tony said. "Just as long as he doesn't try to pay me in beads or blankets."

"By the way," Pete said. "The Colonel said for us to keep a watch on everything going on around here. He agrees with us that's something up, but he doesn't know what."

He didn't tell Tony—without that top security clearance for him, no matter how many personal references he had, he couldn't be told—the Colonel had just now entrusted him with a special "red tape-busting" code word. A code word to be used only during a National Emergency.

Chapter Fifteen

Anna was back in the living room of the strange house. She'd forced herself to finish eating the sandwich she'd fixed earlier, just before the phone rang. She paced the floor, her mind bringing up old memories; places their little family had gone, things she and John Juan had done together, even some of their old arguments. The sun had gone down long ago. She took off her shoes and stretched out on the sofa cushions. She jumped when the phone rang again. It was almost midnight.

"Hello?"

"My heart's own, it has been far too long, and I suffered blows to my head which have destroyed some of my memory. Tell me again the way to our home, so I may resume my sleep on the sweet certainty of being able to fly to you with the morning sun," ibn Billah licked his lips.

That poetic phrasing ought to complete her anticipation. What idiots American women are, to believe such garbage. He stood impatiently at the public phone beside a grocery store at—what was the absurd name of the street? Tramway?—on the outskirts of Albuquerque.

Anna sagged against the wall, her hope and giddy anticipation dimmed by his words. She gave the man on the other end of the phone line the directions.

"Can you remember how to get here now?" she asked dully.

It can't be my John Juan after all. He'd know his way home, no matter how many years it's been. Oh God, why can't you be my husband?

"Yes, my love. I apologize—I probably woke you— really, I just needed to hear your precious voice once more, to assure myself I'm not dreaming. Those directions are what I remembered," ibn Billah continued lying, unaware she was no longer fooled. "But I had to be sure. Al—God forbid I should somehow become lost and waste time trying to get my bearings, when we could be celebrating my safe return. You are sure you don't mind that I don't look as handsome as I once did?"

"My husband, I don't care what you look like now. You will always be *muy guapo* to me, just as you were when you left on your last mission." A tear left a cold trail down Anna's cheek. She hung up the phone and went to the back door; stood outside on the back step.

"Doug?" she called softly.

He emerged from the shadows. "I heard the phone call. Are you all right?"

"I'm okay. Right now I'm numb. I guess it isn't John; that's all I know. Still the same plan and signal?"

"Yes. I wish I could make this easier for you, somehow. I'm sorry I'm right. I wish to God—" he didn't finish his sentence, but pulled her close and briefly kissed her in the shadows. His beard was growing out, and she felt the roughness of it on her cheek as he abruptly turned and moved away.

"I'm sorry," he repeated, and blended into the other shadows further from the house once more.

She went back inside.

Twenty minutes later, she heard a car slow down outside the house, hesitate, then continue up the street. She peeked out from behind a curtain in time to catch a glimpse of some kind of sports car. The light from the streetlights was too dim for her to be sure of the car's color. She retreated to the kitchen after unlocking the front door. Her hands were shaking slightly as she got two coffee mugs out of the cupboard, and poured them full of the hot coffee she'd just made.

She turned to face the man standing in the doorway to the living room.

The left side of his face had a horrible scar the length of it—puckered and twisted, the man's face was a devil's copy of John's face.

"Ah…" the man breathed. "You are repelled at the sight of me. I am too ugly ever to be loved again."

She couldn't speak; face-to-face with this mockery of her husband, she couldn't think for a minute.

What was I supposed to do? Oh, that's right. Offer him food.

"I want you, *querida.* I need you as a thirsty man needs a cool desert spring. Come into my arms and let us go to our bed and pleasure each other." He stepped closer to her, reaching towards her with one thick-fingered hand.

She backed further away from him, and reached for a mug of coffee. "Are you hungry? Can I fix you something to eat?"

"No, I don't want anything to eat, unless it's your succulent lips. I'll go into the bedroom and wait for you there," he leered at her, turned and left the kitchen.

Anna stayed by the counter, waiting for Doug and his back up. Three minutes finally crawled by, measured out slow second by slow second with her heartbeat matching the ticking of the clock on the kitchen wall.

Doug had his Glock 9mm drawn as he slipped quietly through the back door into the kitchen. He put his finger to his lips as he moved towards the living room, warning Anna to say nothing.

Ibn Billah burst through the back door into the kitchen, wearing John Ramirez' old uniform.

"I suspected there might be a trap," he snarled, and Anna saw something glitter in his hand. He began spitting obscenities in several languages as he moved towards her.

Doug Scott was stunned.

That voice! I've heard that voice before! This is the operative who lured my men to their deaths and then checked to see if I was dead too.

Just as he whirled to face the man who was responsible for his squad's massacre, the female officer came running into the kitchen. Ibn Billah grabbed Lieutenant Garner and smoothly cut her throat with the box cutter in his hand. Then as her body slid towards the kitchen floor, he yanked the gun from her hands and fired it.

Doug ran towards the kitchen doorway and into an invisible wall.

Something hit my chest. I can't breathe. I'll be damned—he's shot me!

He stumbled and fell to his knees. *Oh, God, NO! Anna's next!* his mind yelled. He blacked out.

Anna screamed as Ibn Billah seized her by her hair. She grabbed a mug full of coffee and flung the hot liquid into his face.

He didn't let go; instead, he grabbed the wrist of the hand still holding the coffee mug and twisted. She heard the bone break before the sharp pain cut through her. She dropped the coffee mug as her right hand hung uselessly from her broken wrist. The man wrenched her head around to face him.

"You're not John," Anna gasped, trying anything she could think of to distract him. "Who are you?"

He kept his tight hold of her hair—so tight her eyes were watering; leaned down, and licked the side of her face. Anna shuddered. "I planned to show you who I really am," he smirked. "Feel what a real man is like," and he tried to force his body between her legs. She leaned away from him, throwing her weight against his, trying to unbalance him, but it didn't work. Then she heard sirens.

"I wish I had time to fuck you, my pigeon. You would follow me willingly, after you had tasted me. But I can't be burdened with a slut like you."

He pulled a chain around his neck out from where it had been hidden by the uniform.

"Look at this," he hissed. Dangling from the chain was the other half of the eternal love medal she and John had chosen instead of an engagement ring.

"I am Mahmud ibn Billah, descendant of caliphs and sultans," he told her. "Remember me, harlot. I shall return for you someday. And your little worm of a son." He shoved her away from him, grabbed the gun up off the floor; turned and ran out the back door just as the sirens stopped in front of the house.

Anna dropped down beside Doug. "Oh, dear God, that's the man who killed John and now he's killed Doug too," she gasped, trying to find a heartbeat with her left hand. Her right wrist and arm throbbed with teeth-clenching pain.

Doug stirred and said, "What are you worrying about me for? What happened to your wrist?"

Albuquerque police officers burst through both doors, followed by the other members of the Special Ops team Doug had assembled. Anna watched Doug as he sat up.

"You didn't tell me you'd be wearing a bullet-proof vest, you—you –"

"I don't, usually. Besides—" he looked at the body of the female Special Ops officer, her blood stiffening in a puddle beneath her. "Something can go wrong, no matter how much planning you do." He wiped his face with the back of his hand. "Alice Garner was another of the best Ops officers I ever served with. I hope to kill that bastard some day. Slowly and painfully. And I can follow him now. He's wired." It was the third ingredient.

Ibn Billah jumped the back fence and sneaked through another house's side yard, then walked south along a city sidewalk. He turned to his right at the corner and then again at the next, working his way back to where he'd left his old red sports car in the parking lot of an all-night drug store.

I've slipped past them, he thought, his ego not realizing the Special Ops team let him get away. *And now I look like one of them, in my uniform.*

Once back in the driver's seat, he drove unhurriedly back to I-40 and headed west out of Albuquerque. He'd get out of the city and then call Salim Makhadi. His coup of a Special Ops officer's uniform and military ID in his wallet would be reported to even higher ranks of *al-Qaeda*—perhaps to the Director himself.

He made the initial call and then waited at the same phone booth inside the Diamond B truck stop on the west hill. The phone rang twice, then stopped. When it rang again, he answered. Makhadi's voice curled into his ear, sweet as any incense smoke. He had been rewarded in a small way already. His would be the signal honor of telling Jabar al-Rimi when to launch the little crop duster planes from Flagstaff towards the power plant outside of Joseph City and Hoover Dam.

Chapter Sixteen

Jabar al-Rimi panicked upon hearing about the power outage in California.

"Allah aid us and show his merciful face to us! We should have launched just before the snowstorm!" al-Rimi wailed. The other operatives were slumped in their chairs, the lights turned low in the big meeting room at the office of the Christmas tree farm. "We shall be torn apart by jackals in the desert if we foolishly did not perform our actions as they were needed. Even though we received no signal, no phone call, no email—we shall be blamed if the power outage in California somehow lacks effect."

"Uncle Jabar," his nephew timidly interrupted. "Could we not launch tomorrow? If we take out our assigned section of the other power plants, it will still throw the infidels into panic. And we can say we did not get the signal in time because the snow snuffed out our transmissions."

Al-Rimi's face cleared a little. "True, we have had some trouble with receiving signals in the past. Perhaps we can in truth say that we did not receive our orders, and still be a part of the glorious blow against the Americans.

"We must clear the runway of the snow and scrape away the dried grass underneath. We have headlights on the tractors; we can clear the runway under cover of darkness. All may not be lost. We shall launch our glorious assault at dawn, just as the noble savages, the ones they stole this country from, used to do. My nephew, you will have a special place in Paradise, of this I am sure."

The boy flushed and hung his head, pleased at his uncle's praise. Rarely had he ever heard any.

It was a crisp early winter day and the sun was behind him. Ibn Billah was enjoying his new role as messenger. He always appreciated a chance to be the one issuing orders. It was now his duty to tell the cell in Flagstaff to launch their planes in two days' time.

The uniform from the American Special Ops pig has already engendered a reward; I am the favored son because of my initiative and bold plan. The snow slowed him a little; the highway officials had been cautious and closed the road. He'd had to stay overnight in Gallup.

Ah, well. They will still have plenty of time to launch; they are to be ready at all hours now, merely waiting for the one word to start the next strike.

And he possessed that one precious word. He drove on west, unaware that Al-Rimi's nephew at the tree farm had neglected to put a new cartridge in the fax machine. The machine could print nothing, not even the carefully-worded signal ibn Billah sent from his motel in Gallup, and so they were unaware their messenger was on his way.

Sierra slammed the phone down, disgusted. "Even having an uncle who's a general doesn't help. How in hell am I going to get out into the field? I need to be out of this office where I can keep an eye on these *hijos de putas.*"

He started to pace the office, then stopped as a thought hit him. *We're all supposed to be "non-military" now, without a real paper trail. But I could cut some "Permission to Operate on his Own Initiative" orders so I can get a truck, too, and follow Mr. Perfect Braun and Turncoat Aslam cross-country. That'll work. I know how the military fancy crap is supposed to read, so I can get the papers worded right. I'll have to have a purchase order for a used rig—I can't wait a month to have every fancy luxury loaded into a sleeper for me. By God, I'll be on the road in a week!*

119

Tony shook Pete's shoulder. "Hey, Pete, we got trouble! Wake up—something's going down at the Christmas tree farm, man! I went out at dawn, just to check, and they've got the planes out and warming up, getting ready to launch!"

With a pen, they drew a quick map and plan for everyone participating on one of the restaurant tabletops.

"You came bobtail, didn't you? Then let's go bobbin' for terrorists!" one big trucker slapped another on the back. The entire café was emptied of all but the waitresses and cooks in minutes.

Mazman Frank kicked his Harley into action, the powerful cycle sounding like a snarling wildcat as he roared out of the parking lot, Wolf right beside him on an equally huge hog.

Cab doors thudded closed almost as one sound. Drivers watched their dials cycle and cranked the engines. Revenge was going to come on eighteen wheels this time.

Nobody drove foolishly, but they all drove skillfully and fast—faster certainly than the men at the tree farm could ever anticipate. Now the common enemy of America had a face and was within striking distance. Every trucker rolling knew he was facing not only his possible death at *al-Qaeda's* hands, but the planned deaths of innocent civilians once again.

A few miles outside Flagstaff, the rigs turned off on a raggedly paved side road. A lopsided sign said "Christmas Tree Farm, one-half mile." The motorcycles were at the far end of the tree farm parking lot, circling and swooping, distracting the foreign men as they watched the "crazy Americans" perform riding stunts from their office windows.

But they couldn't be distracted for long. Fueled and ready for flight, small crop duster planes were lined up in three rows across a newly-mowed field.

Four of the logging truck cabs drove to the edge of the clearing and stopped, still out of sight of the tree farm's buildings, big engines idling. Men climbed out of the cabs, took logging chains from storage and hastily hooked them onto the trucks, side front bumper to side front bumper. Drivers rumbled their engines as one rider swung up into each of the four bobtails, now hooked together into two pairs of eighteen-wheeled destruction. The other truckers started running towards the Quonset huts and office, carrying tire thumpers in huge fists.

"Funny how many loggers you can pack into a bobtail," Steve said as he ran with half a dozen other drivers.

"Hell, who do you think taught the bed-buggers how to pack?" Robbie answered, and laughed.

The office door burst open and the *al-Qaeda* soldiers stopped, staring at the sight of yelling, swearing truckers racing towards them. They turned and ran back into the office building, slamming the door just as the first wave of enraged truckers reached it.

The chained bobtail pairs drove right into the lines of waiting planes, catching wing tips or landing gear in the chains and flipping the small aircraft. As the planes were tossed and shaken, the flying bomb mixture of chemical fertilizer and diesel fuel slapped together. Two loggers stood on the back of an empty flatbed, lighting and throwing small explosives into the middle of the mess of planes like they were flipping lighted matches.

Explosions and violent bursts of flames peppered the field. Paint scorched off the truck cabs but the drivers didn't care. Eight of the planes—one third of the force—were now in flames.

They swung their rigs around, watching the would-be pilots in the remaining planes hop out of their cockpits and literally run for their lives, heading into the forest around the air strip. A second pass should take out nearly everything still flight-ready.

A rifle shot snapped through the air and the bullet tore through a driver's window. He slumped, hit and hurting, but managed to slip-seat with his passenger, who let out a Rebel yell and jammed the accelerator down.

"You bastards! These birdies ain't gonna fly!" he bellowed. "Hey, Kenny, you all right over there?"

"I'm good, David—they just hit my shoulder. Take 'em out!" And the rigs leaped forward almost as if they were living, vengeful animals.

The slammed door didn't hold back the angry truckers at the office building, especially after they'd seen that rifle barrel thrust through a broken window pane and the gun fired in the direction of the bobtails. Three of them kicked in the door, while Tony grabbed the rifle and jerked it hard, pulling the sniper's face into the jagged broken glass. He yelped and dropped the gun.

"This one don't sound like he needs more air," a plaid-shirted trucker remarked as he swung his tire-thumper into the belly of an *al-Qaeda* recruit.

"Oughta make it safer for the delicate little spotted owls now," another said; dragged up a cursing, kicking man by his collar, and punched him again.

The airfield was a scene from hell as trees caught fire and stood as flaming torches against a gray winter sky. What had originally looked like a WWI airstrip had been smashed into crumpled wings and puddles of flaming fuel.

Inside the office the fighting was bare-knuckled as the angry Americans seized every operative within reach.

"Save something for the Feds to question, men!" Pete Ramirez yelled over the noise, as he grabbed Jafar al-Rimi, owner of the "wretched tree farm" and shoved him out of his office into the main room.

Now they could hear sirens, lots of them, even over the roar of the flames around them and the continuing explosions. Tony ran up to Pete. "A couple of the bastards jumped out windows and got away from us. They ran into the woods, heading the same way as a handful of the pilots."

Then they heard plane engines turning over again.

"No!" Pete and Tony yelled at the same time, and ran out of the office door towards the fifth bobtail, idling at the side of the burned-out airstrip, driver behind the wheel, waiting to run where he was needed. He revved up the motor as they leaped up into the cab.

Shifting gears as smoothly as if he was on a highway, the driver pushed his rig through the woods, down another narrow winding road and onto an even smaller secondary airstrip.

Six previously hidden small planes lifted into the air as their rig rolled to a stop at the edge of the field.

"Damn!" Robert Cooley said. "If I'd known about these planes, guys, I would've run 'em over."

Pete and Tony stood outside the cab, fists and jaws clenched, watching the planes gain altitude. Pete climbed back in.

"It's okay, Robert—nobody knew they had reserve planes stashed. But let me get on your CB and see if there's any way to scramble some Air Force planes and get those bastards shot down—quick."

Just as ibn Billah got to Winslow, smoke suddenly poured out from under the hood of his car and the radiator blew. He strode to the nearest auto shop, swearing under his breath in five languages.

The mechanic drove them both back to the disabled car in his tow truck and looked under the hood. He shook his head. "Mister, in the wintertime, you got to add antifreeze so's your engine stays runnin.' We'll have to pull this radiator off and try to plug the holes. We don't have anything that'll fit a car this old. Especially a sports car."

"How long is this going to take?"

"Well, we've got other customers ahead of you."

"I must get to Flagstaff! My father has had a heart attack!" Ibn Billah's face was a grayish shade of purple.

"All right, I understand you need to hurry. We'll pull this radiator right now. You just go sit down in the waiting room and we'll get your car running again."

Ibn Billah paced the floor.

Am I going to be thwarted by mechanical failure now? He clenched his fists. *No, no, by Allah! I will not let this stop me! There is still time to get to Flagstaff and launch the next wave on my order! I shall have my first mention in history!*

Chapter Seventeen

Three hours later, he was back on I-40 and speeding towards Flagstaff. Suddenly there was a huge flash of light to his left. Another one a few seconds later was more to his right and he felt his car shudder momentarily. "What the hell is going on?" ibn Billah asked aloud.

He drove through the late afternoon and twilight, finding the turn-off for the farm by the old sign hanging on a fence post beside the Interstate.

The farm was deserted and desolate. His headlights showed large burned areas of dried-up grass and broken planes, upside down or with their wings snapped like twigs. Ibn Billah got out of the car.

"What have those fools done? They tried to launch on their own initiative and screwed it up?" His voice rose nearly to a shriek as his fury grew. He cursed in his native tongue until he ran out of breath. Then his shoulders sagged and he went back to his car. His hand trembled as he turned the key.

"They can't blame this on me," he said aloud. "I wasn't even here. I have to find a phone." He remembered seeing a small truck stop on his way to the farm, so he headed in that direction.

Inside the restaurant, he saw several pay phone booths, then realized he had no coins with which to make a call. He pulled a five-dollar bill from his pocket and went to the register. As he stood there, the front door opened and a rowdy bunch of truckers came in. The cooks and waitresses cheered them as they entered.

"We heard about some of the fight! Sit down and tell us everything!" Belinda called, cupping her hands around her mouth to be heard over the uproar. She spotted the foreign-looking man at the register.

"Sorry, officer, I didn't see you standing there," she apologized and went to ibn Billah.

"I need change," he thrust the bill at her.

"Say, if you're part of the military here to arrest those SOB's who tried to sabotage us in our own backyard, you go right ahead and take all the change you need. And I don't need any money back." She gave him a handful of quarters and went running back to the knot of truckers. "Just holler if you need more."

One trucker had his arm in a sling and was telling his story to the cooks, who were hanging over the counter.

"But Kenny, what happened after you got shot?"

"Did you save the bullet?" someone asked.

Kenny held it up. "I sure did. This little beauty means *al-Qaeda* missed a kill!"

Other truckers were telling the townspeople crowded into the truck stop what had happened at the tree farm.

Ibn Billah sat down in the phone booth but didn't close the door. He felt sick. *Somehow the infidels smelled the operation and snuffed it out the day before our launch date.* His stomach burned from the acid pouring into it.

"You mean they actually hit the other crop dusters with missiles from F-16's?" He heard a low voice as two truckers walked by, the first going to another phone booth, the second man heading to the men's room.

"Yeah, didn't you see the flashes of light? That was the guys from Luke, taking out *al-Qaeda's* bully-boys. The last wave was evidently heading for Hoover Dam, to turn off the electricity for everything from Lost Wages to half of Shaky Town." The trucker who answered had a black eye and his shirt was torn. "Hell, we had a great fight going."

Details of the trucks being used to flip the planes— "Like burgers on a grill," a cook said admiringly—were being told as ibn Billah staggered to his feet. His fury made

126

it hard for him to breathe, but he managed to walk through the restaurant and shove the door open.

"Whoa!" Tony Parker Chino said, catching the door before it hit him in the face. He looked at ibn Billah's purple face and quickly stepped back. "Here, officer, you come out and I'll go in, how's that?"

The officer said nothing, just shoved past Tony and hurried out in the cold night to an old sports car in the parking lot. Tony stood still for one heartbeat and then turned and ran back towards the motel, the pins in his bad ankle rubbing against bone.

I just left Pete in the room to grab a heavier jacket, he was thinking. *There's no way he could've gotten into a uniform and gone into the truck stop ahead of me—what in hell is going on around here?*

As he slipped on patches of snow, he realized the ID tape on the uniform had read 'Ramirez, J.' He reached the room door and beat on it.

"Pete! Pete! Where are you?"

Pete opened the door while shrugging into his jacket. "I'm right here. Where would I be? You look funny—what's going on?"

"I just saw your brother John!"

"You can't have! He's dead!"

"The uniform said 'Ramirez, J.' on it and he was just in the truck stop. He's got a really ugly scar running down the entire left side of his face!"

Pete reached out and grabbed his friend's shoulder to steady himself. "Omigod! That's the man with the scar we were briefed on! Oh, God—I've missed him! I've got to call the Colonel!"

An hour later, alerted by a quick phone call from Colonel Daily, Mike and Emad pulled their rig into the motel parking lot and went to meet Pete Ramirez, who was beating himself up for not having seen the *al-Qaeda* operative masquerading as his dead brother.

"I would've killed him!" Pete said to the older truckers while walking the floor. "I would've strangled him with my bare hands!"

Emad pushed him into a chair. "Calm yourself. Major Scott knows where this man is at all times. Your dead brother's very uniform is still serving his country: a GPS transmitter was inserted into a seam where it won't be noticed. John Ramirez has reached from his grave to help stop the next strike."

Pete put his head in his hands and hunched his shoulders. "I'll never forgive myself. Why couldn't I have been the one to see that bastard instead of Tony?"

"Because you would have done just what you said you would do," Emad continued, his voice hard. "You would have killed him. And then we would have no idea where he was supposed to report next. Allah saw that your hot-headedness would have struck him down, so he had Tony become a witness instead of you. Now we can follow this human filth and possibly prevent yet another disaster."

Mike cleared his throat. "I'd like to hear some more details. The Colonel said this *al-Qaeda* operative has balls—he's checked in at another motel in Flagstaff; he must think he's invincible. But we've got people watching the room already. We need to remember to give this guy his head so he can run."

"And lead us to the others," Emad finished Mike's thought.

Tony stood up. "Pete, the next time you see this guy, I promise you I'll help you take him out. Remember my ancestors knew some really slow and painful ways to kill someone."

Pete raised up his head and tried to laugh. "You're right, Tony. Are we gonna start carrying some big jars of ants around with us?"

"*Amigo,* if that's what you want, that's what we do."

The four men walked to the truck stop restaurant. Once inside, Mike and Emad sat on the fringes of the now-dwindling group and listened. The adrenalin rush was wearing off for most of the truckers, and they were starting to head back to their rigs or rent rooms to spend the night.

"You know what's really kinda neat about this whole thing?" one asked as he paid his bill at the register. He continued without waiting for someone to reply. "The people who live around here see us as heroes now, instead of dirty, foul-mouthed truckers."

"It won't last," a voice came from one of the back booths. "But if you want to go and marry one of the town girls, Randy, now's your chance." Several truckers laughed and went out the door. Their footsteps crunched in the snow still left on the parking lot.

The cooks looked at each other. "We gotta get this place cleaned up. We're supposed to be serving dinner in an hour."

The four men sat in a booth as the truck stop's next crew shift came in, still somberly thinking about the last two days and the latest attempt on America.

"I still don't get it," Mike said, finally, clutching a coffee mug with only grounds left in the bottom of it. "Why do they want to hit just ordinary, average Americans? What do they have against us?"

"It's not a holy war, either," Emad replied. "The Prophet told his followers to live in peace with all religions. And in the beginning, there were even Jewish settlers among Muhammad's people in the small villages from which he taught and preached."

129

"It's personal with me, now," Pete said. He still hadn't gotten cleaned up from the fight; his face had a smear of grease on it and his knuckles were crusted with blood and dirt. "I'll kill that son of a bitch, for no other reason than looking enough like my brother to blacken his name."

The men all looked at him, and then Tony nodded. "The only good terrorist is a dead terrorist. Let's go get cleaned up and catch some sleep. Won't you guys have some new orders in a few hours?"

"Actually, our orders remain the same. Continue searching, continue trying to find cells before they activate, continue trying to stop these bastards before they succeed in bringing our country to her knees," Mike answered. He liked the young Native American; he had guts. "And we've kept regular log book hours, going cross-country. We can easily push on west after a couple hours' sleep ourselves. I'd like to see if we can't join some of the other members of our team. Ty and Errol were supposed to be finishing up in Phoenix, weren't they? Why don't we drop down I-17 to Phoenix and catch them at the Diamond B? And Dino was going to meet us outside of Quartzite, of all places."

"We would do well to meet and proceed west," Emad agreed. He felt it in his bones—that was the direction they needed to travel, and his translations seemed to bear that out. He glanced around the restaurant, blinked, and looked again at a dark-haired woman leaving the restaurant with a take-out meal.

I'm beginning to imagine things, he told himself. *I would almost swear that woman was Maryam. But she died in Saddam's prison too. It must be the altitude here—the lack of oxygen is causing my mind to produce peculiar visions again.*

Rising from the small prayer rug, which was carefully aligned with the East, Karem stood in the faint light of the dawn.

We launch in only forty-eight hours. Those fools in Flagstaff nearly destroyed the entire mission. But as the Director told us, the stupid Americans will quickly subside into their sluggishness, feeling we cannot strike again so soon. And then, that so-close glorious day within my grasp: when the sun rises, I shall pluck ripe dates and savor sweet nectars as I stroll in the lush gardens of Paradise. Inshallah!

Chapter Eighteen

Ty and Errol were leading the way west, far away from being home in Virginia with their parents for Thanksgiving weekend. Mike and Emad followed the van line truck, their Environmental Solutions logo prominent on the sides of the tractor cab and trailer in the last rays of the setting California sun. Dino came behind them, driving an ordinary SUV. He was keeping an eye on a small black car that had been somewhere within sight range of his vehicle for several hours. Fifteen minutes behind the group, Pete and Tony were marking off the miles in Pete's faithful old clunker.

Emad had no time to be admiring the desert area surrounding Interstate 10; he'd glanced up from his notes briefly when Mike commented how much the sparse vegetation and sandy soil looked like Iraq and the Middle East. He was haunted by several recurring phrases in the original papers about "meeting the caravans, as the caravans supplied the goods for the bazaars," and "the revered place of birth of the Prophet." In one set of papers alone, the caravan phrase had been repeated over twenty times.

That has to be significant, he mused. *Is it a signal for a date or a time, if they are employing the military system?*

The two trucks came to a group of truck stops, huddled together like an oasis beside the traffic lanes. Over the CB, Ty and Mike agreed to stop for about twenty minutes and then continue. Errol called the others on their cell phones, to tell them to take a break too.

"Emad, aren't you going to get something to eat? I've got to stop and at least grab a sandwich," Mike interrupted the scholar.

"Just bring me one also," Emad answered.

"Are you getting closer to figuring out the next strike?"

Emad sighed, and rubbed his eyes with his hand. "I wish I could say that I am. At one moment, I think I have solved the puzzle. Yet I look at another passage and find that I have not."

"Get out for a few minutes and get a breath of air," Mike climbed out of the cab.

Emad closed his notebook and moved his small desk, which had been perched on his knees for the better part of the day.

Outside the truck, he faced east and said his prayers, then slowly paced the perimeter of the parking area while waiting for Mike to return. He wasn't hungry—another coughing fit had left him feeling a little weak and he stumbled as he walked beside the Cars Only lot.

An adolescent youth with a beard was unloading some small boxes from an old pickup truck parked nearby. "Pure *Jojoba* Oil Hand Lotion" was stamped on the boxes' sides. The youth saw Emad and jumped, nearly dropping the carton in his hands. He carefully set it on top of the others and walked hurriedly to Emad, his smile glowing beneath a scraggly beard.

"Are you our messenger?" he whispered to Emad. "I bear proudly the name of our blessed Prophet, Muhammad. I wait most eagerly for the chance to serve him in glory here before waking in glory—there." He looked past Emad, who had stopped walking and stood waiting to hear what the young man had to say. He turned almost in a circle then, openly looking to see if anyone was watching them.

Raw recruit, Emad thought. *Bet on it.*

Emad nodded at Muhammad. "You do well to be cautious," he told the young man, quietly.

He cannot be more than—what? Seventeen? What is this chance at glory he is whispering about?

133

"I am here with—friends—who have joined our cause. Is the meeting place still the same?"

Muhammad nodded eagerly. "Just look for a sign along the highway; it will direct you to our farm."

Emad laid his hand upon the youth's shoulder, causing him to lean down towards the older man.

"I shall see you soon. For your own sake, do not mention you have seen me. You passed the test, by recognizing me, and being brave enough to speak with me. But others at the farm will not have had this opportunity, and they may envy you."

Muhammad's face was flushed with pride at being singled out from the other workers at the *jojoba* farm. "Thank you, revered messenger. I shall return to our farm and wait your arrival."

Emad nodded, and walked back to the truck as Muhammad hurriedly carried some of the cardboard cartons into the truck stop.

Mike came back to the truck balancing several sandwiches and two hot cups of coffee. He found the truck engine already idling and Emad with his head bowed over his notes again, searching the pages as fast as his eyes could read.

"Didn't you even get out for a few minutes?" Mike asked, irritably.

"Start driving!" Emad commanded, without looking up. "And tell Ty and Errol to look for a sign along the highway which says something to the effect of "*Jojoba* Products" or whatever. We shall have to mark the exit for it, drive past it, and then notify the Colonel so he can help plan our next move."

Mike had already stowed the coffee and sandwiches and was putting on his seat belt while thumbing the call button on the CB. He relayed the message from Emad to Ty and Errol, and then called Dino on his hands-free cell phone as Environmental Solutions rolled out of its parking place.

"Can you follow that old pickup that's parked five cars away from you in the lot?"

Dino chuckled. "You're about to see a dinosaur tiptoe. And it'll give me a chance to shake a little car that's been glued to the bumper for a while."

Mike pressed the speed-dial for Pete next.

"What's going on? What do I tell these guys?" he asked Emad, as the phone rang and Tony answered.

"So far 'what's going on' seems to be a remarkable coincidence," Emad told Mike, who filled Tony in on the group's movement and Dino's shadowing, then closed the phone. "But I must watch for that sign."

Not ten minutes later, Emad pointed to a freshly-painted wood sign hanging on the wire fence along the Interstate. *"Jojoba*—10 Miles" it read, with an arrow pointing to a narrow side road.

"Good thing you figured we'd have to go on past," Mike commented. "There's no way we could take an eighteen-wheeler down that cow path."

"Dino will have to catch up with us, too—that road is deserted, and any vehicle moving on it will be noticed instantly," Emad said. He grabbed the CB, told Ty and Errol to take the next exit, and repeated the message for the other three men over the cell phone.

"Next exit!" Mike called, and hit the right turn signal. Out of the corner of his eye, he saw Emad's face turn gray.

The exit sign read, "Mecca."

A Note from the Publisher

The mention of products and their trademarked names in this manuscript is to provide reference and descriptive information for the readers. There is no intention of infringement whatsoever upon these trademarks.

www.ingramcontent.com/pod-product-compliance
Lightning Source LLC
Chambersburg PA
CBHW021112130626
46554CB00002B/659